The Husband's Dilemma

The Husband's Dilemma

Nicole Stansbury

CARROLL & GRAF PUBLISHERS
NEW YORK

The Husband's Dilemma

Carroll & Graf Publishers
An Imprint of Avalon Publishing Group Inc.
245 West 17th Street
New York, NY 10011

Library of Congress Cataloging-in-Publication Data is available.

ISBN: 0-7867-1300-3

Printed in the United States of America
Interior design by Simon M. Sullivan
Distributed by Publishers Group West

for Grant

Acknowledgments

With love and deepest gratitude to my friend and agent, Loren Soeiro, of the Peter Lampack Agency, and to Andrew Lampack and Peter Lampack, for their confidence and support.

To the amazing Tina Pohlman of Carroll and Graf, for her intelligence, humor, and creative vision.

Thanks also to Sandy Blanton, Rema Dilanyan, Wendie Carr, and Nate Knaebel, for providing invaluable technical and research assistance.

With tremendous gratitude to Roni Wilcox and Alison Jones, for helping so much with Otis and Jack during the writing of this book. This book would not have been possible without you.

Finally, with affection and thanks to my writer's group: Dawn Houghton, Julia Corbett, Sara Zarr, Debora Threedy, Rachel Borup, Lee Mortensen, Jan Nystrom, and the darling Kevin Avery.

Contents

A Woman
Sweeping

TIM, THE ROOFING GUY, has a favorite joke: *Why did God give women legs?*

So they wouldn't leave snail tracks.

Tim clomps up the stairs with one regular shoe and one platform shoe, and though he has a sweet smile, he is off-putting immediately with his theory of planes exploding and/or disappearing at the hands of the U.S. government. Plus he can never stop telling me how happy he makes his fat wife in bed. Happy, happy, happy! And I get to hear all about it. He is out to prove something to me: that even though he has a twisted spine and one leg too short, his fat wife begs him for more. That's what I get to hear about, and this I do not understand. I have a clean home, one with an immaculately white kitchen floor and a bed with a dust ruffle. My husband and I have to move all of our many pillows, four king-size with shams and then the two we actually use, onto the tapestried bedside ottoman each night

I

before sleep. I use Crest teeth-whitening strips as does my husband, Luke. We have two beautiful small children who wash before and after meals and who understand the importance of an early bedtime. It is very important to us to pay for things in a timely manner and keep a nice home and take vacations twice yearly, once in a locale with snow as we're both good skiers, and then once on the beach. We're good clean people, we pay our taxes and like our privacy. We're great neighbors. We take white plastic bags each time we walk our two golden retrievers, Zoe and Babe, so as to clean up after them. And so I cannot quite understand how things have gotten to this point. I can't understand how it is that somehow Tim is in my house and in my face every day, telling his dirty jokes. And then how, because I do not want him to feel bad, I pretend to find them funny.

What I want him to do, merely, is finish roofing the house, as promised some six weeks back by the foreman, or sales manager or whatever he was, of Kimball and Company Roofing. I chose them from the yellow pages because their ad said Thirty Years Service and Satisfaction, and also because their name sounded respectable and male and trustworthy. For the same reason, I choose to shop at craft stores named for example Michael's or Robert's, as opposed to JoAnn's.

This is a true bias which I am admitting to.

One of my highest priorities when seeking out and choosing a roofing company was the workers themselves. Finally after several snafus I've learned not to just go with the cheapest guy, not to just select someone randomly with a small ad in the classified section of the local newspaper. Let me tell you, and I had to learn that one the hard way. I had guys who never showed, guys who showed up with booze on their breath, and more than a few who thought my wanting to hire them for this or that home repair meant they thought they were entitled to let their eyes have a walk all over my body. Then there was the plumber who I caught inspecting the contents of my medicine cabinet. So now I only call the ones with a Yellow Pages ad.

I can tell by the way the men conduct themselves what kind of workers they will be. If they are pleasant but not needy, if they simply and merely type in numbers and figures and then tear off a pink sheet with their signature and business card stapled on, then I know we'll be a good match. As they are not up in my face and we both appreciate efficiency. This was how it was with the roofing company, Kimball and Company, and imagine my pleasure when I saw the foreman's car out front, a nice clean and newer model maroon Ford Taurus. He came up the walk slowly, wearing a starched button-down shirt and wire-framed spectacles. I liked him immediately. You could tell he had a wife who gave him plenty of food and affection. This is pretty much my perfect vision of a blue-collar worker. One with a calm demeanor, his SpeedStick working, his cell phone charged. And then how he sat right down at my kitchen table to produce a cool and calming price estimate and allow me thoughts of all my happy future days with a new solid asphalt-shingled roof on my house.

He was such a perfect vision when he appeared six weeks ago that what I did was, I started sweeping. Sometimes this happens. I get nervous; I want to make a good impression. I mean I want him, Mr. Kimball or whatever his name is, to know that I appreciate my own husband who traipses off every single day to work. To know that I am not a freeloader.

I am very, very far from lazy. I think, seriously I do, that a clean kitchen is very, very important!

He asks me a few curt questions, then goes to stand outside and look up. Then he comes back and works up more numbers. He doesn't even say yes to a drink of water, and this almost never happens. I'm so happy, so sure I'm going to go with his company, that I keep right on busily filling the dustpan.

I think maybe I like the way it makes me look.

Like, frankly, sweeping the kitchen floor makes me look femmey and docile. Kind of like Snow White. My head's down and I'm off-center, right? Going back and forth a little with my hips, not dancing or anything, heck I'm not saying that, but I'm saying if you think about it that a woman sweeping, well, for once she's off the defensive, not reaching for the pepper mace here, I mean the plain fact is that even with more or less perfectly strange men in my house and most often camped out at my kitchen table with Palm Pilots and clipboards and cell phones and all that, the plain fact is that often as not my back is turned and my head is down and ripe, if it came over any one of the repairmen, for bludgeoning. So I guess maybe the sweeping thing is a way of trying to say I trust them. That I don't think they're going to give me a jacked-up estimate or a crappy cooling unit or anything. Sweeping is my way of showing the Mr. Kimballs of the world that I'm impressed.

Also I guess I'm beginning to think it's possible that even a woman such as myself, with hips spread from babies and my hair cut short in a bob that curves nicely and non-threateningly on either side of my cheek, can look attractive while sweeping. My haircut is designed to give the impression that I am a mother who does things, who returns calls, who drives her children places. I look capable, is what I'm saying, but even still I am not without desires!

I mean for one thing, my feet are bare. And I have always had extremely pretty feet. Plus the pile of dust and dog hair and broken crayons can be daintily stepped over. I can lift one foot, and daintily brush off whatever crap might have adhered there. I do this a couple of times for the benefit of Mr. Kimball—who, God bless him, does not even look up. I'm thinking that he must be getting some very, very good sex at home. God bless Mrs. Kimball!

I take a stroll over to the fridge, where I have each kid's color-coded school and activity calendar. Mr. Kimball is wrapping up. I'm trying to catch a vibe, trying to detect even a whiff of yesterday's tar under his fingernails. He tears off a pink sheet and slides across a reasonable bid.

"Will you be doing the work yourself, then?" I say.

"Me personally?" That gets a smirk. He taps the pink receipt a few times pointlessly, like he's reconsidering the bid. "We send a crew," he tells me.

Which basically means Tim.

Let me say up front that I do not have anything against hand-icapped people. I never, even remotely, park in their spaces.

But what I mean is, Tim is Mr. No—Currency. Mister man with a heavy wife at home and two small children who have inherited his twisted back and bum leg. But he knows, finally, plenty about my roof, and you know one thing I like about Tim? That he really seems to care, like, *personally*, about this job. He uses so much tar goo on all the seams and around each of the skylights that you know if he were working for say McDonald's, or even Wal-Mart, they'd for sure fire his butt. He clomps around all over in my attic and all day long, staying late, holding his leg propped off to the right of his body like a rubber one. He has a quick sweet smile and he always rinses his coffee cup in the sink.

For the first week, it's like this. Then a couple of other guys show up, and for five days running it *is* an actual crew up there, hammering and tearing off shingles and blaring country–western music. The job is supposed to take only five days but on Friday I get a call from Mr. Kimball, or who I thought was Mr. Kimball, who as it turns out is actually Mr. Jefferson the sales manager. He tells me we will be "into next week." That's the message on my machine, anyhoo. When I call his cell phone I get a recorded message.

They're still at it by Wednesday of the following week. Things keep happening. Tim shows up with two different guys, and one lets his eyes take a walk. I can never decide how nice to be. Am I supposed to hide in here like the spoiled white wifey? When I see one guy, Jeff, drinking from the hose, it makes me feel bad enough that I ask them into my kitchen. I don't usually do this kind of thing.

THE POLICY I HAVE IN THE PAST INSTITUTED, WITH REPAIRMEN IN GENERAL:
—don't invite inside
—DO occasionally take out healthful snacks and drinks
—don't ask about their love lives
—don't distract them with conversation
—DO give encouragement, such as a "thumbs up" or the "okay" sign
—DO establish healthy boundaries

This policy is one I've devised and had in place for some time, as I have a life here. It's just that things get confused because yes, I have a job here, I do things, I keep this whole doggone house cleaned and stocked with supplies like carpet-stain remover and batteries and birthday gift wrap and Goo Gone. I am saying I take this job seriously. I'm saying—because I am the freeloader, because I do not produce actual legal tender for this household—that it makes me work like I'm really earning six figures. I am the ass-kicker housewife! I am the boss! And this also applies to repairmen who show up to work up estimates on their Palm Pilots. But it gets confused because even with all my power, even with being one heck of a great mother who cares about such things as making paper crafts with my kids and using a cookie cutter each and every time on the slices of bread when doing sandwiches, I somehow look like The Lady. And this in spite of other professional child-rearing gestures: for example, the color-coded calendars for each child's recreational activities like soccer Monday, chess club Tuesday, karate classes Thursday, neighborhood pool party Saturday two P.M. please bring candy for the piñata. Yet the repairmen seem to think I'm the Available Lady in spite of these signals.

And in spite of other deliberate demarcations, like chopping my hair. See, by chopping my hair I thought that that right there would draw the line, this new haircut making me look no longer virginal or sexy obviously but instead just *capable.* And I have many other ways of sending that clear message. That I am now a mother and the ass-kicking queen of this household, which starts you know it buddy the minute you step foot over my threshold. Because in this household I know what is going on, I know when the milk expires and when the car is due for an oil change and which pets need what shots and when the bills get paid and when the library videos are due, and I know morever that I am in this brief lull only, when the repairmen show up, the lull between noon and three P.M., 3 P.M. being when the kids come home from first and fourth grade, respectively. So that perhaps it looks like I am a woman of leisure sweeping; but believe you me I am anything but leisurely or relaxed.

When the repairmen drag out chairs and sit at the table to pour out their hearts, and they do, I hear about wayward kids and wives and sometimes bankruptcies and boo hoo, do I look like their therapist? I guess I do. I'm there with a smile on my face, trying to be a good listener, trying to be a people-pleaser, and all the while the clock is ticking and they have no idea. That even this instant I'm bracing myself for the onslaught, dirty dishes and scattered socks and shoes and backpacks and above all the querulous demands of tiny people, whom I think would like very much and most of the time to take over this household, to secure me to the beach with strings and pegs. Now just lately the first-grader has for example been referring to me as *stupidious*. They want things, and I love them and want to be a good mother, and they want tiny maddening things, cheese cubed and not sliced, and orange cheese but not white cheese, and the blue sippy cup with the green sippy cup lid only, and one ice cube please, and the yellow shirt and certainly not the purple one. And so when the repairmen also need these small attentions, also need my love and constant listening, I think of other things I can do, like no more tight jeans and only linen drawstring pants.

No heels, obviously, ever.

Very little makeup.

I am at work here, darn it, and not here for some repairman to ogle. I am hard at work here and this means, when you are going to give me an estimate, do not look at my chest or even, as I am sweeping, my heinie. All this belongs to my own nice husband who listens to me and pays the bills.

And I just certainly do not want to be a freeloader to my husband by doing things such as sitting down or even, like some other wives I know, using their time to go off and get a massage, or making themselves pretty with dangly silver earrings and linen clothes and chunky sandals in order to go off to some restaurant and meet another lady who looks the same, for lunch. This is not my thing at all. Even as my hard-working husband exhorts me to slow down and put my feet up and take it easy, to at least occasionally get horizontal so that he can then lay atop me, rarely do I do this thing as always I can feel the clock still ticking and know in my heart what it is that needs to be done next. If I do not for example get vertical and go move clothes from washer to dryer, the one son's soccer uniform will not be dry for tomorrow.

But with all this said, still with the repairmen guys I am forever walking a fine line. Like when that one guy wanted a sandwich and I would not make it. The tile guy. I would not make him a sandwich, just construct it, because I did believe he could do it himself. Because I said to him I have things going on, making a sandwich is just stacking, there's bread and then mayo and then on slap the ham and cheese, and *voila*. I saw no point in doing it but try telling *him* that when he said, could you maybe just fix me something quick? And do I look like his mom? Do I look ready to help? And when I said here's everything, here's ham and cheese, when I tried to explain that it was *only just stacking*, well, he left. So depressed. So depressed that he punished me by not returning to fix the tile for four days. And all because there were people such as me in the world, who on principle would refuse to make their tile guy a simple sandwich.

My point is, Tim is taking too long with the roof. Kimball and Company needs to wrap things up.

The work runs into the second week, then the third.

Do I look like family, do I? Tim comes inside without asking now, just comes right in when he's tired and uses the remote to channel-surf. Right there in my living room. It is so hot up there that he can only work into late morning, I do know that. And crew? What crew? Tim seems to be the only one left. Then, and I have seen him, if he continues to work into the afternoon, in the heat, everything up there gets so miserably hot that he vomits. This I have witnessed myself.

Meanwhile Kimball and Company has cashed my check, and the two times I went in to speak to a manager personally, well, both times they were "at lunch."

"At lunch." Good one.

There are two things about my husband: he works long hours and he's a Nice Guy. He doesn't mind so much how long the roof takes. So any complaining is up to me, and I am being driven crazy by this thing.

Day fifteen: Tim has asked if he could nap in my house.

On account of the heat, he explains. Like say work from six A.M. 'til noon and then work again from 5 P.M. until 10 P.M. And siesta in between.

At first I don't get it. *Nap?* I say.

Because I'm ready to puke all the time up there, Tim tells me. It gets so hot by about eleven and then you know, I have a commute. It's twenty-five minutes home and twenty-five minutes back so what I thought was, if I did nap here. In between.

Where?

Well, anywhere. Your bed. The couch.

Your bed. He really says that.

Now, I know about the heat. I know the whole roof thing sucks. I know I'm down here underneath, air-conditioned, and one time I dropped off a check at Tim's house and got to see his screaming limping kids and the TV on too loud and how his wife did crafts so that there were little cuttings and scissors everywhere. I saw how she rolled her eyes at stuff he said, but I tell you what, still there is absolutely no way he will be napping all during the day in my house.

For how many days? I say. Because I have stuff going on.

And when Tim sleeps he is, above all, meaty. He is a mouth-breather in a damp white t-shirt and his legs, which he often flings atop my satin duvet, look like the legs of the largest Billy Goat Gruff. I could *so* live without Tim. Then there was impending doom on the Weather Channel, and so on a Wednesday Tim cut out early, saying *no worries.* And because I can be stupid, because sometimes I think all I really am is the check-writer, and because furthermore the man I call my husband was at this point eating peyote in Mexico with a bachelor friend and descending by burro into some canyon, I chose to let it be, let it be, and I got the kids bathed and put to bed and then I myself drank a full bottle of Chardonnay and fell asleep watching the *Daily Show with Jon Stewart.* And at two A.M. I woke to the sounds of water overhead, a sound like rain pouring down on some parking lot in the sky.

Truly: it was heavenly up there in the attic, as if there had never been a roof at all, and water coming all around the sheets of plywood haphazardly covering the largest areas between joists, and it was amazing to see. It was raining straight over the place where the future canopied king-sized bed with 360 thread-count sheets was going to go, and also in the nook where I was going to set up an easel and do my art, and though I knew that this was merely and technically a rather large setback only, still I totally freaked out, yelling and screaming first into Mr. Foreman's answering machine and then right at Tim. Because of course I knew that according to the law eventually everything would get fixed and that tomorrow would bring sunshine. But for now I am a hopeless know-nothing with her husband's checkbook only, as solace.

So here stands Tim at two thirty A.M., looking up at the wet sky like this is no big deal at all. I'm shrieking and crying. Tim, it seems, has been yelled at a lot in his life. So now he does everything patiently. He limps over here, patiently places a bucket there. And I'm hitting speed dial over and over, trying to get through to Mexico.

It was such a spectacle! Like a backdrop of TV rain. Like computer-generated lines of silver.

How can this be? I kept saying to Tim, hitting speed dial.

I just needed to seal it a bit better in places, Tim says finally. It's not a big deal, he goes on. This is actually how it works. You do a roof, then you wait for the first rainstorm so you know where to go back and fix. That's what you do.

This is not what you do! This is not! I'm stomping my foot; I sound like Dr. Seuss.

Tim patiently spreads a tarp over some of my stuff. It is abundantly clear, however much Tim is trying to act like Mr. Professional Man and keep his cool, that once his boss finds out, Tim's ass is grass. The cold air is making me shake. I am wearing only my bathrobe.

Tim does what he can with another tarp and then some

plastic sheeting. But finally he just perches himself on a toolbox and watches. There are rivulets and drops and pools and puddles and I don't know how this can be, I don't know how this can be. Tim puts his face in his hands. Then he gets up, comes over, and puts his arms around me. I punch him, a puny fist to the chest that makes him step back. But then he tries again, keeping his head down and his arms open, and he smells good and I like that his bum hip means he has to lean into me. The point is he's sorry, and who else do I have to blubber on right now?

Fuck Mexico so much.

And anyway a woman sweeping, and then a woman weeping, a woman with a big ass and short hair and a guy with basically only one leg, so what.

It is all so really confusing! I mean do I look like his wife, or what? I do not even remotely like the guy.

Still.

The
Activist

His wife, Perry reflected, was the kind of woman he once would've lost no time in getting rid of.

She was hunkered over there behind her menu, dark and sad in her foxhole. There was so much darkening! Her mood joyous, her mood hateful. And now that she was pregnant again it was worst of all. He did things like tie her shoes for her, trying to chip in.

They had invested badly. It was only three thousand dollars, but still. Within two weeks it was worth ninety-eight dollars, and now she wanted to try again.

A tried and true company, she said. Maybe Microsoft.

I have political problems, Perry told her. Not Microsoft, no way. Bill Gates. Maybe Greenpeace? Something like that.

So fine, forget Microsoft. McDonald's.

McDonald's! They slaughter cows, they destroy the rain forests.

I don't care about cows, she said. They're stupid, I don't care, we're hypocrites, we take Jake there all the time.

True. Jake was four. It was one of the hills of parenthood they'd died on, McDonald's. There was much moaning, much protesting, by the time the kid was one, but they lived in a cold climate and there were few options. The mall? And so with the world snowy and gray, disgusted with themselves, they'd folded and gone to Playland. Even the pediatrician had warned against it! That was where kids picked up hoof-and-mouth, he said. And in spite of hoof-and-mouth and the rain forests, they'd gone anyway.

Perry always ordered the McFish. Or whatever it was called. On account of his being a vegetarian.

They fought about so much! How she seemed to dislike him! When he announced it in restaurants to the waiter: I'm a vegetarian, is there something you'd recommend? So that his bitchy wife would stare him down. How she hated that! His *announcing*, she said. Couldn't he just order? No one cared! But they did care, Perry thought. And sometimes they had suggestions—though, he had to admit, not often. They were eighteen-year-old boys; they wore single earrings and goatees, and most often peered perplexedly at the menu over Perry's shoulder, scanning with an uncertain finger right down the page and stopping, with relief, at Salads.

And here they were. Behind their separate menus again, and fighting.

All right then, General Electric. Lightbulbs, stoves.

They're a military–industrial complex, he tells her. Another company. Anything. Just something we don't feel bad about.

I don't care about that! She cried. It's half my money! I'll do what I want with my half, how's that? I'll invest in whatever I like, I'm still working, I'm still making money for another few months anyway. You invest your half in whatever you want. I'll do mine, I'll do McDonald's, I want the kids to have some savings, I don't care, I don't care. They're *cows*. A field of shoes, Annie Dillard once called them.

Didn't she see it? Everything was at stake, everything was changing. Once he'd worn dreadlocks, once he'd worn Guatemalan pants with bells at the cuffs, once he'd gone to the Nevada test site to protest, and there in a sleeping bag in the wee hours he'd lain with Kelly, who was freckled and olive-skinned and very soft, and in the morning they'd stood up and dressed and kissed and collected their signs. And now his wife had to spoil it all, point out the hypocrisy of everything. Like her job in life was to make them both feel shitty about themselves. Everything about her was edgy and angry, unlike soft soft Kelly.

But he was not stupid. He knew a deal when he saw one, and his wife was smart and pretty and ironic and he loved her, for all of her nervousness and bad temper. He had, Perry reflected, a gift for seeing the best in people, for seeing people not as they were but as they wanted to be seen; and however trite it was, the thought moved him to take her hand.

And what did she do then? But bait him.

So then, Microsoft, she said.

No no no no no.

Yes! This is not about you! She slammed the menu down. People were looking. I'm worried we won't have money for their college! We just lost their college money in two puny weeks on some stupid-ass computer company we didn't even fucking bother to research the stock history on! We're stupid! We don't know how to invest! It was our whole savings!

When she could not shut up, as she could not shut up now, Perry would take his food and quietly move to another table: a sunlit corner booth, freshly wiped and sunny and entirely his. There he went at his sandwich carefully, feeling her humiliation at his back. He plucked the pickles from his deli sandwich. This was how it was, being a vegetarian in a small town; they thought a veggie sandwich just meant a sandwich with the meat removed, leaving him a pile of sickly lettuce, thin and milky-looking tomato slices.

He had married her, in part, for her obstinacy. At first her hard-headedness had looked sexy, and they'd had discussions about it: how in her mind men seemed to long for women whose brashness and physicality reminded them of themselves: saucy women, snowboarder babes who sassed in public and had the pleasure of telling off men, especially the ones who wanted to fuck them. He had concurred. That was certainly partly why he'd chosen her. But now he saw, after only a few years of marriage, how quickly her sassiness could turn to meanness. It cowed him, it angered him.

Maybe: and maybe more important: his wife had once been interesting.

Once she had been a painter.

And moved over canvases, and had flung paint and had not even picked up the phone when he called. And wore overalls, and took her whiskey straight, and made him, well, basically: kind of beg for her affection.

The paintings—really—were not all that good. But her squatting over a canvas, and staying up until three A.M., painting and painting and listening to the Ramones: now that was a sight for sore eyes.

Now, his wife writes letters.

This instead of painting. She scowls, and things frighten her, and more than anything what frightens her are the products that get *recalled*—the *baby* products that get recalled— and she obsesses, surfs the net, types in *child safety, baby safety*, and is furious to discover that they *actually own certain recalled products*, or anyway owned them until just that moment: the moment of their going in the trash, the moment of the next letter being composed.

Dear Sir/Madam:
Recently I discovered that your bath book series, marketed as the Pat 'n' Peek bath books, contain the toxin phthalates. Since I feel that you are of genuine goodwill and that your products are sincerely set forth, I will try to articulate my complaints in patient and reasonable terms. This product could kill or at least greatly sicken either my existing or soon-to-be-born son. And if it couldn't actually sicken them, it sickens me, right to the core and most especially at three A.M., at which point I must awaken my nice husband so that he can assuage my fears. I understand that these books are no longer being produced by your company; all the same, you must be aware of the fact that, via donation centers and doctor's offices and the homes of unsuspecting daycare providers and for sure probably in libraries—these books are still in circulation. I implore you, please do whatever you can to rid the world of your books containing phthalates.

What do you think? She'd ask him. At the end of nearly every day, she'd composed another. Each evening she wanted his opinion.

Very Martin Luther King-y.

Did they think she was an idiot? That was what she'd ask him. Did they think, because she was now the *homemaker*—did they think she was *stupid?* That they could charge whatever amount of money for unsafe products, for toys that either didn't work or broke easily?

Yesterday's letter:

Dear Sir/Madam:

I recently purchased a Special Agent set (containing dart gun, whistle, baton, and badge) for my son, aged four. Please know that within about three minutes of getting home from the store, the suction cups popped off both darts, creating incredibly sharp projectiles and infuriating me and making me feel, like I'm made to feel every day by this parenting job, like the Bad Mother. Since I feel that you are of genuine goodwill and that your products are sincerely set forth . . .

And now their three-thousand-dollar investment, gone awry.

He works at his apple pie, provided quietly by a gaunt woman of few words—the one who brought the apple pie, she would never lay into him, never make a scene in a restaurant—and thinks how she is silent at his back, thinks how probably she is so spiteful as to be investing at exactly this minute, on her cell phone, in some company even more hateful than he could've ever even begun to imagine.

After a while he sneaks a look back at her. She's eating, he's happy to see that. He's a good guy who cares about whether she eats. For real.

But he'd married a career woman. A painter of enormous canvases who'd stood, in the old days, in a black turtleneck, sipping Chablis from a plastic cup and looking ill at ease beside one of her paintings. She'd worn maroon lipstick. She'd looked cross, and kept her arms folded. The gloomy painter. His heart had gone out to her. His future wife, depressed and painting and drinking furiously, his wife who had a studio. Back then she'd practically hurled the blobs of paint at the canvas in a sort of bachelorette's gloom and rage. All this long before the kids had come along, of course.

Now, well, to give you an idea, she ordered her swimsuits from Lands' End. Hey, not that she wasn't still lovely! But I mean: what was with the shelf bra? What *was* a shelf bra? Why did it matter? One of her chief appeals was her teenaged boy shape. Tiny breasts, a lax drinker's waistline, little butt. *And whomsoever needed a shelf bra, it was not his wife.*

In it—frankly—she looked weirdly rounded-out, wrongly bolstered, the elastic of the legs bisecting her thighs unattractively, and sorry to note that she had her own mother's stumpy legs, pale and blue-veined, sorry to say that since she'd taken a year of unpaid leave from her painting/teaching job, finally having been given a little lark from life and bill-paying, the whole plan being for her to paint and spend more time with Jake—sorry to say that now she was using this time to either order shelf-bra swimsuits online or write these letters, incensed.

And today had started with yet another letter.

What was it she was trying to accomplish? Her heart, now that she was a mother, all the time on her sleeve regarding such things. Because she was writing about windows. No, *screens*. Exhorting Embassy Suites, in case they cared, to do this thing and place screens on their windows—which now they didn't— and now since last August exactly two more toddlers had plunged to their deaths. *How many more children must die?*

she'd written, meaning it. And wanting what exactly? Fifty percent off a future suite?

But no.

This is not what I'm trying to tell you.

She *meant* all this, had clipped articles about toddlers falling, and then falling again. Had gone so far as to research which hotel chains provided screens on their windows. A regular Ralph Nader, his wife. A regular activist.

He wasn't making fun. He wasn't. He loved her. But what of her paintings, what of her creative energies and ambition? It's the painterly wife whose mouth he wants to feed. Not the—not the letter-writing wife. He sneaks another look back, sees her hunched and scribbling. What's up with all that? What's up with all the time she spends organizing? Because, guess what he found in a drawer the other day? A "Chip Clip." It was what it sounded like, and sure, you could make an argument. The Chip Clip shut the chip bag, so as to guard against waste and staleness—that was reasonable. But it was something a *grandmother* would have on hand, wasn't it? Was he being reactionary? Was he being cold?

He tries to think of a company they'd both agree on, but the three thousand was exactly all they had, the smallest of nest eggs, now squandered. He's stalling, and finally turns in the booth, stretches out his legs to wait for her to make eye contact. She's pregnant; he needs to remember that. Needs to remember that right this moment she's basically all hormones, something with very sharp teeth. She'd as soon drive him from the den, he's sure of that. But they're married humans with manners, and so they do other things, like call each other names and move to separate restaurant tables. It's terrible, he thinks sometimes, to be what they are: trapped primates, living in tall buildings without screens on the windows, trapped sad humans who scribbled and quarreled and kept right on reproducing. She would find this funny. She has a great laugh. He misses her. He sends her a telepathic message: *Hey. Come on over here.* He sends it again and again. And then in fact she *does* slide in across from him, swigs from his coffee without asking, flashes him a peace sign.

For a moment, the babies of the world recede. His wife feels like a friend again, an ally. So what if they lost some money, so what if the world's basically astoundingly unsafe, so what if they made a mistake and now have to start over with the college fund? Shit happens. But his wife seems to be formulating an opinion of the restaurant's high chairs, stashed off to the left behind the coat rack. He sees that they're rickety and old—though *vintage* is the word he would've used, back in the days before he'd had to consider whether to plonk his own kid in one. Way way way way way back in the days before they were parents. Can they ever just have a moment to themselves? Ever just not have to worry? But she's already starting a new letter over there on her side.

Leap

(for Deb McGhee)

ONCE ON TV I saw a stigmatic. This particular one was chanting and all aquiver, her eyes slitting out everything but bliss while the other believers, clay-footed, looked on. The camera zoomed in on the rust-colored marks on her palms, and I thought it was fancy that the girl was earnest enough to give birth to the spots. I for one have been enough of a yellow-bellied chicken liver to give it up only at night, so that the next day my friends point, drag their fingers sadly along the flesh saying, what happened? What happened here? They are remarking on swatches of green—sometimes on my shins, again on my forearms—dotted dark around the edges, like sliced kiwi fruit. I can't think to say that my body is basically taking the rap. An imbecile, fertile and bone-laden, horny and ridiculous, this body couldn't spot a metaphor for anything. It's the bargain fruit, like the rotting but fragrant bananas whose capture my mother used to put us kids in charge of, the ones piled in an extra cart at the end of the aisle.

I'm trying to say how lately I've been noticing people in pieces: or anyway, with pieces gone. There's a girl at work, a janitor, who smiled lopsided at me the other day, and you could see the difference. Once she'd been a student of mine and these days she was someone else, her eyes liked to look off to the side and her speech was looser in the limbs. I don't know what must've happened. Maybe hit by a car. Maybe fallen from a motorcycle. And now a whole different person.

Then I saw a lady with a suddenly bad hip. She didn't used to walk that way, so that you have to be amazed by the survival going on in the world. She went up on one stiff foot in a white leather sandal like it was dancing. Her husband, I noticed, had learned to walk slower. He strolled now with his hands behind his back, taking some time to stop and smell the roses, since he had this new girl. And when my mother gets her headaches, words on a page just disappear. Just fade away and collapse on either side, until all she has left is a syllable.

You have to wonder, after that kind of parting out, what the point is. *Memories, like the corners of my binder,* is what my mom—mad at Barbra Streisand because my dad thought she was such a dish—used to sing. And later the melody would break her heart every time, since she thought of it by then as their song. When it came on we'd try to whip past, and wonder about it when she insisted, when she had to sing along and cry, making it look happy. It was my mother teaching me not to be vigilant, to forsake her so she could sing, *what's too painful to remem-HEM-ber, we simply choose to-HOO for-HOR-get.* And her face was more beautiful than I can speak here, and her rendition always brought down the house.

How can I explain? I have suddenly in my life, this heart. She has a crooked nose, a drawl. She is sulky, she bites, her hair hangs over her cheeks, she is essential. I have this theory that she walks like a hound dog, which is to say in a hurry the way such a dog might be, roaming a neighborhood, restless and hungry. Across from me in booths she looks for outs, for driveways or an alley; and hauled close, her nerves are shot. You can feel both of us jangled, breathing hard, so that anyone with any sense would know to separate us. We are terrified of each other, see, and crazy in love. Yesterday, having noticed one of the greenish nighttime love bites, my newly beloved—to make a point—lowered her mouth to my shoulder and gave me a hickey. A laying-on of tongue. Not that the woman on TV, who let the spirit seep so cornily through, was anything but fabulous. But yesterday, for the first time ever, I had the nerve to watch my girlfriend walk away. She got small, and when she waved, her hand in its white glove looked to be floating. *Hallelujah!* I wanted to say. Because if you could see for one instant the way she moves through this world—her face dipped and attentive, her hair sliding; her gaze off and away, scanning for ships and lovers and tiny black silhouettes—you would know my shipwreck, and the gesture of sheer stupid faith such a girl would inspire.

American
Bush

IT WAS MY IDEA to drag him to American Bush. My idea, totally.

We'd been in the kitchen rolling quarters down our noses, and suddenly for some reason it seemed like a good idea. I'd never seen exotic dancers before and I guess I thought it was a way as much as anything to demonstrate that I was no longer insecure, something obviously Ian has accused me of, well not accused but enlightened me about, the fact of my insecurity, and he would know. He has a master's degree in psychology.

Ian was one of the most unique people I'd ever met. He was pushing forty, but the meditation and vitamins and herbs and all that stuff, the ginseng and bee pollen and tantric yoga, made him look ten years younger. He was skinnier than I was, and wore his hair and fingernails long. He'd met the Grateful Dead. He'd been to India three times. He took longer then I did getting ready, and changed his outfits even more often, and had these amazingly intense deep-set eyes. He gave a mean massage. He wore his hair all in tiny braids.

Ian's friend Mike was over. He's a pretty nice guy. But I hate the way he *dances*. On the dance floor, Mike becomes someone else. He has looked at me, a friend, with smoky unrecognition before pelvic-thrusting meaningfully my direction. He does this with all the ladies.

Anyway we'd run out of San Clarita merlot and somehow the subject came up and here I thought it was just going to be this great opportunity to prove something.

"Honey, just the sound of it makes me nervous," Ian said. "I think you have some sort of agenda. I think you're acting out about something and I'm not sure what."

"I'm acting out about not having any more merlot," I said. "My agenda is to see some pasties because I don't really know what they are or how they keep them sticking on."

"It's just, you know."

"Know what?" Mike said. I do like Mike. Except for the way he dances.

"Never mind," Ian said, and took my hand.

"Don't you even want to see them? They're women. Strange women, dancing for you and only you and practically naked and they might even give you a lap dance!" That cracked me up. My own words cracked me up. Me so funny, me so drunk.

Mike drove his own car, in case some woman ended up wanting to come home with him. He always did this.

I love Ian. I LOVE IAN VERY MUCH. Which also meant that I was afraid, at all times, that one day he'd wake up and realize what a pipsqueak he was with. But truly, I thought the whole stripper thing could work. Clubs were my terrain. I'd gone to dance clubs practically every weekend before I got with Ian. I'd even learned a few stripper moves way back when; moves which possibly, with a few more beers, I would bust out tonight.

But: Ian did not like to drive. And he was bad at it. On the way to the bar I got the usual lecture about the need for mass transportation in our city. This segued into a discussion of petroleum waste, and the need for people to use fewer resources and practice family planning, overall. One thing I appreciate is that even though he's older than me, Ian's never gotten stuck in a marriage. He's healthy that way. He thinks people should be independent and not just have kids and get stuck in the suburbs. I might want to have kids someday, but it's refreshing to be in a relationship where the guy just doesn't want to treat me like his property. Plus Ian and I do everything fifty-fifty. We split everything right down the middle. Car insurance, rent, everything. Which is fine with me. I think women should pull their own weight.

"I might be a tiny little bit worried about this," Ian said, and looked over.

"About what?" I rolled down my window. On certain nights, I wanted a cigarette. This was one of those nights, but Ian hated seeing me smoke.

"Well, I mean. I just think you do have some issues. With insecurity. I don't think it's your fault at all. I think you're wonderful and beautiful. But you know, I don't know how you're going to feel around a bunch of naked women. I mean I guess as much as anything, it just makes me nervous to have you there with me looking at naked women. Do you see where I'm going with this?"

"It's going to be funny! I've never seen such dancers as these! As those that we will see!"

"Okay," Ian said. "Just promise not to get mad at me. I am just a guy."

• • •

We found Mike and had shots of tequila at the bar, then got a table next to the dance floor. I was thinking about what Ian said and if I was going to get freaked out and then I remembered how usually when I'm in public with him, and if another woman has such good taste that she hits on him, what I like to do if this doesn't sound catty is just go up and give him a big kiss. Not to be possessive or weird but just to show them that it's a great night and we're there together and that it's all good. That's the way I protect myself and also show him my love. Plus I wasn't worried about having to compete with some stripper. From what I hear most of them are gay anyway, either that or living with a mess of kids in some trailer. Right?

That was actually what I was thinking.

So then, it was like the Real World washed up onto my shore. And my whole hilarious life with Ian and everything in it got swept out to sea with the bottles and plastic straws and disposable diapers.

What happened was that Luna took the floor.

One thing, Luna worked out. Everything was perfect. Everywhere it should be soft looked soft, and everywhere it should look muscular there was a tan and loveable and firm area. Luna did a slow song. I think the singer was George Michael. Then a fast one, where she swung her hair in an arc and jiggled and pumped her tiny hard butt.

"Do you have any money?" Ian asked me at the end of a song.

"Do you want me to go get us more drinks?"

"No, I mean for a tip."

"To tip *her?*"

"Yes, to tip her," Ian said patiently. "Are you doing okay?"

He held his hand out my direction. He was having a hard time peeling his eyes away.

"I have a buck."

"A buck? Do you have your ATM card?"

"A buck is reasonable."

"A buck might be kind of an insult," Ian said. "Give me your card." Another song started up. Luna figured out we were talking about money when she saw me pass him my debit card. She squatted directly in front of him and pinched her own nipples until they perked up.

"I really don't think they're going to have an ATM in here."

"They do." The music had started up again, so that Ian had to yell. "Over by the pinball machine." I shrugged to show that I was clueless about the location of the ATM, unlike him.

"Where?"

He pointed elaborately and mouthed it: *please, money.*

I took a break in the bathroom, which was far and away the quietest part of the club. Making drunk bar friends was always good, so I bummed a cigarette from one woman, Lynette. "Thanks," I said. "I have to go outside to smoke. My boyfriend hates seeing me do it."

"Mine too," said Lynette.

"Mine three," said Lynette's friend, Richelle. They were both wearing blonde hair extensions. "It's so weird how guys hate to see their girlfriends doing that."

"It's like a control thing," Lynette added.

I took Ian the twenty, and he surprised me by tucking the entire thing down the front of Luna's thong. Then he turned and gives me an exuberant kiss. "Are you okay with being here?" he shouted.

"I'm great, but did you have to give her twenty bucks?"

"What?"

"Did you have to give her all twenty?"

Ian frowned and looked confused. *Too noisy!* he mouthed.

"Twenty! Why twenty!"

"Have a heart!" Ian said. The music faded out. For a minute we could actually hear each other. "You can tell from her stretch marks she has kids. I don't want to just act like some pervert by watching her dance and then not even helping her out. She looks sad. Don't you think she looks sad?"

"I don't see any stretch marks."

"Don't you think she looks depressed? I should talk to her on the break. I should see if she's ever seen anyone."

I finished my beer. I would've tipped her myself of course, but more like a *five.* I wanted another drink, but my balance, according to the ATM, was $81.02. *Minus* the twenty. "I don't think she looks depressed. I think she looks *happy.*"

Ian was concentrating on her thong. "No," he said. "You can just tell. She's putting up a good front, but she's sorrowing."

"Is that a verb?" I said.

"What?" The music started up again, a pointless *thrump thrump thrump.*

"It sounds like a word from, like, Old Yeller."

"What?"

"Forget it."

"*What?* Too noisy!"

"Forget it!" I pinched his butt and then made another trip to the ATM. Then I detoured to the bar for a double shot of Jim Beam; by which point, absolutely, I felt fine. Mike was at the bar. He slouched into me for our conversation, putting his mouth very close to my ear.

"Any luck?" I asked him.

"They're all lesbians. As usual. You know, if I were Ian, I'd be right here with you, not drooling on Luna."

"She's the lesbian." That's what I'd decided to tell myself to keep from getting jealous. I had to plain ignore his other remark. I was afraid he'd ask me to dance.

"All women are lesbians," Mike said, wetly and near. "Wouldn't you rather date somebody close to your own age?"

I kissed him on the cheek. "Good-bye. Knock 'em dead. Must fly, Sugarpie."

"How come all women hate bald guys, anyway?" Mike called after me.

Back at the edge of the dance floor, I gave into an impulse to yank up my top and show Luna my boobs. A few people on the sidelines applauded. She laughed, I laughed.

Go Luna!

She was wearing a silver thong and had glow-in-the-dark stars and planets stuck all over her bod. I think stick-on stars are a swell idea!

A shooting star shape, naturally, just above her crotch.

"That's great as hell!" I said. "Check it! Let's stop at Wal-Mart on the way home! That is so totally cool. I swear I'm gonna get some. I could just glow and prance, glow and prance."

"Shhh," Ian went. Things were quiet. Luna was poised. It was a quiet part of the song.

"Seriously it's so cool!" I exclaim, and somebody across the bar went *Hush!*

Luna started to slowly hump a spangled scarf she was holding between her legs, and all the guys there, including my Ian, looked the same way, doggy and glassy-eyed. I was here, I was real. I had a sexy bra and a cervical cap filled with spermicidal foam already high up in my body. I was drunk but prepared. But Ian wasn't much noticing me at this moment, and suddenly the thought of that just made me so *sad*. Why did I have to be such a sad person? Why did I always have to want something other than what I had? Why did I just always have to want home and safety? I wanted to be married, I wanted to be home and in front of the TV with my Ian. I couldn't stand the look on his face. The way just watching her seemed to have brought out what was essential, his hunger and horniness. It wasn't *fair*.

Now Luna was sucking on a lollipop. A Tootsie Pop, actually. I couldn't figure out where she'd gotten it. Not like she had pockets, right? Ha ha. But anyway she was sucking and licking that thing for all it was worth. I laughed again. "Nice," I said. "Nice! I'm going to try that one on him later! Good one!"

The lollipop disappeared between her legs before popping back into view. People clapped when they saw that, like it was some great talent. Then Luna tossed her hair and sort of growled and threw one leg up on the bar and guess what, stepped *over* the bar, dainty and straight-legged in frilly socks, and landed in Ian's lap.

And. Oh my.

Ian *moaned*.

Had I not done this for him? Had I not done *praise Allahs* at the mat of his wildest fantasies, and at four in the morning, when I'd preferred to have been sleeping? But Luna arched her back. She was looking at me, giving me in fact an entirely cutting glance, making a point. Like maybe she thought I'd been making fun of her stick-ons.

Then Luna raised the lollipop to Ian's lips and gave him a meaningful look.

I'm absolutely crazy about Ian—that's the thing.

I love him.

We're best friends.

And it's not like I wanted to be with some guy my age, a goateed undergrad who was madly in love with his own skateboard and said *dude* every other word. But I guess what I'd been hoping these last few months was that Ian and I were on the path to somewhere better. I mean bars are fun and all that, but soon enough I wanted to get on with life, maybe try to move from our apartment into a house where we could have a vegetable garden. And I'd never tell Ian this but I get practically weak in the knees every time I walk past Gap Kids in the mall. I know if we had a kid it would be cute. I'm just a sucker for those tiny chenille sweaters and baby high-top Converses. I can't help it.

I nudged him, but it was like Ian and Luna, alone in the universe. His eyes were practically rolled back in his head, he was so ecstatic.

Ian seized the lollipop and stuffed it in his mouth.

A while later, Ian went out to the car to wait for me. I knew that because he'd passed me on the way out, giving me and the cigarette and my friends such a look of such disdain that I flipped him off. I spent a few minutes watching the car darkly from where I was, a few cars over, before lighting another cigarette.

"He looks sorry," said Lynette.

"Yeah," said Richelle. "He actually looks super-sorry. But also kind of mad."

"He can just wait his ass off," I said. "He can just fuck my ass."

That sent Lynette and Richelle about into hysterics: *fuck my ass!*

"We all just better, like, drink tons of water before bed,"

Lynette said. Every time she exhaled, she flapped one hand to wave the smoke away from her face. Then the three of us just watched Ian's car.

"What's he doing in there?" Lynette said.

"If this car's a rockin', don't come knockin'!" Richelle said, and she and Lynette snickered. Then Mike appeared. "Another perfectly good night, wasted," Mike said. "Me, and the night."

"I am so grossed out," I said. "I don't even want to have to sleep next to him tonight."

"You can spend the night at our apartment," Lynette said. "We have a futon."

"Does that include me?" Mike asked.

"Really? I swear I might."

"You *totally* can," said Richelle.

"You guys are just great," I said. "I mean it. I just totally love you."

"Call us tomorrow and let us know what happened at least," Lynette said. "And drink lots of water. Plus, take some Advil."

"*Don't* tell me good-bye," I heard Mike say as I was walking off. "Fine. Be that way."

"I did nothing wrong!" Ian said. "This happened because of you." The strip joint was behind us, a few blocks back, a tiny building that cupped Luna like a heartbeat or a flame. And further back, earlier in the evening, was the secure Me. The one who'd had this bright idea in the first place. Now I was clusterfucked. There were too many strands to untangle: the way our potentially perfect and hilarious evening had started, with my original idea to go watch strippers and prove something, I knew now absolutely not what; and then the strand of Ian's thing with the lollipop, and my getting pissed off, and two more shots of tequila to make my brain and all of the evil colliding thoughts stop, just *stop*, so that I wouldn't care and would no longer be pissed and above all things so that I wouldn't start, the way I absolutely knew I was going to start, the very argument we were having now.

"It's because of you! That was just sick!"

"I did nothing wrong."

"I'm sorry but I mean okay, my idea to go there was a bad idea, I'm sorry, that was stupid. But why the fuck did you do that! And you should've seen, you should've *seen* the stupid look on your face."

"I did *nothing*. I'm just a guy!"

"Except suck some Tootsie Pop she had up inside herself! How fully disgusting is that! You're going to give us both syphilis!"

"That is just uncalled-for. Not all exotic dancers have diseases. That's just mean."

"Whatever! You sucked on her stinky lollipop!"

"I knew you'd think that way. I knew you'd think that. That is so like you, to just think of every other beautiful woman as a sex object." Ian turned on the radio, hoping, I guess, to drown me out.

"Um, excuse me?"

"I feel *sorry* for those women, is what it is."

"You have got to be kidding if you're going to play it this way." I stared out the window. I was so confused by this line of reasoning that I felt my own mouth hanging open. "This is how thoroughly baffled I am," I said, and pointed out my own open mouth of slack amazement. Ian missed the whole thing. He was too busy being in denial.

"Look: if you were an exotic dancer, if you were one of those women, I would've done the same for you. Okay, maybe I shouldn't have put it in my mouth, but what the hell else was I supposed to do? It would've hurt her feelings, okay?"

"So you just didn't want to *hurt* her *feelings?* Excuse me, am I on Candid Camera?" I couldn't stand when he pointed out what a hugely compassionate guy he could be. One time, his compassion made him give a backrub to a single lonely woman at the bar, and then buy her a drink. Then there was the compassionate time where he told a woman at work that he was single to keep her, as he explained it, from feeling bad about her own status.

"So is that why you had to use my debit card?" I asked.

Ian slammed on the brakes, pulled over, and found the meditation mat he kept rolled up between the seats. He took it and walked off into the darkness. A minute later, I heard him chanting.

I rummaged under the seats, looking for a bottle. Sometimes I found something. But not this time, so I dug out a piece of Sugar Free gum instead. All I really wanted was for Ian to come back and maybe make a joke, like say he was ready to stop and pick up some Listerine. That was all it would take. I had the spins, and closing my eyes made it *much* worse. Finally I gave in, which meant letting myself puke in the gutter. Ian's chanting stopped briefly while I retched. Then he took it up again while I searched the glove compartment for Kleenex, which of course there were none. That seemed, suddenly, like something very wrong with my life: I was unprepared. *We* were unprepared. I was insecure, and Ian desired other women, and in the meantime there was vomit crusting at one corner of my mouth. The kind of woman I'd always wanted to be existed only in my imagination. She always had Kleenex and maps and anti-bacterial wipes on hand. She was a mom, and she drove a Volvo and her glove compartment was stocked with antibacterial wipes, goldfish crackers, a pen, a blank check, a tire gauge. She kept fresh flowers all around the house. She took care of everyone, the husband and kids and small animals, and was not just sexy but deeply *necessary*.

Ian came back. He rolled and quietly stowed the mat, then slid in. We drove for a while and then he said "I want you to know that I wish you no ill will."

"Thank you," I said. "Back at ya, baby. What flavor was it anyway?" Then I laughed. There were at least two beers in the fridge, and I was thinking it would be nice to get home and crack those and try to salvage the evening. In my next life I also plan to drink a lot less booze, but until Ian and I are over the hump it's about all that's left me.

"Don't you bring it up ever again," Ian said. "I'm forgiving you. That's all that should matter to you at this point."

"I can't bring it up?" See how I am? I couldn't shut up. All I had to do was *shut up*.

"I told you, and I'm not telling you again, that whole lollipop insult is beside the point, in fact we both know it is not *even* the point, I just felt bad for her. I felt bad for her! I'm just that kind of a person. So don't turn it into something else."

"What did I turn it into? I'm seriously so totally confused!"

"What did you turn it into? *What did you turn it into?* I don't like stupid people, Julie. You know that. And I don't like stupid questions. That is one of the fundamental evils that gives rise to human suffering, stupidity, and that's what I'm seeing here."

"I just thought it would've been nice if at the bar you hadn't stuck that thing in your mouth. That is what I'm saying. That was just an icky thing that I did not appreciate. And I really didn't appreciate how much you tipped her. Okay, that's all, I'm sorry, I'm sorry, I don't want to fight all night, I never should've suggested it in the first place, I'm sorry."

"So you think what I did was inappropriate?" He was using his calm therapist's voice on me.

"Yes, I most truly did."

"That's because you couldn't understand her," Ian said. "You just thought it would be so great to go there and look at those women and laugh at them, didn't you, you thought that would make you feel so proud of yourself and superior. And I mean I didn't expect to do that myself, but believe it or not, I'm glad I did. She obviously feels shitty about herself. And I just think you should think about that."

"Okey doke, artichoke," I said. "Whatever."

"And you're just a little smartass."

"So, I just want to make sure: this is all my fault, right?"

"Read my lips," Ian said.

The next day, Ian meditated in the living room for like, three hours. I read a book on the back porch, trying to stay at least a little bit mad at him. But the day wore on, and my dignity wore thin, and I got sad and then sadder until finally I just missed him. I missed him. If he would toss me even a tiny something, the very tiniest of peace offerings, I would take it.

After a while he came in, wearing his black drawstring-waist yoga pants. He did a few neck rolls and leaned against the desk. Then he exhaled slowly, inhaled mightily, and exhaled again. I was a little red sailboat about to be blown out to sea.

"You need to learn to take me at face value," Ian said. "You need to learn that I'm not the kind of person who has motives."

"Okay."

"But you thought last night I was being, as you put it, 'inappropriate.'"

"Whatever, Ian. I shouldn't have dragged you."

"'Whatever.' 'It's all good.' What is that? What does that mean, when your generation says those things? Those statements mean nothing."

"I'm just tired. I don't want to fight with you anymore."

"So you think I took that lollipop because I was turned on. And not just because I felt bad for her."

"I guess I kind of did think that. But the point is I don't want to fight anymore."

"But you think I did something wrong! Instead of seeing it from my point of view, as an act of *generosity*."

"Okay. You're right. I'm selfish. You sucked on a Tootsie Pop fresh from her twat because you were moved by her. Okay. All right."

"See, and when you use that tone, I just feel like you test me to my absolute limit. You test me to my absolute limit. *This is your fault*. This is your fault. If you hadn't dragged me, this never would've happened. And it disturbs me, quite frankly. That you need to sexualize her, make this something sexual when it's about something else. I just find that really alarming."

I was tired. Really, I just wanted to lie down. Okay, Ian. Okay. You're right.

I opened the kitchen cabinet and found the peppermint schnapps and chugged it down, all half-a-fifth of it, and his eyes never left me. I saw pity there. Once again, it was me, me, me. My fault. And all because I'd grown up in a crazy household, with a crazy alcoholic mother actually, making me the crazy bad one. The one with the diagnosis.

And really, I was never entirely sure whether or not it was true. Really I wasn't. It seemed so possible that I was the problem.

I *loved* him. I loved him so much, it about broke my heart every day. That was almost the worst part. If I'd loved him even one iota less, I'd have the decency to stay mad at him. I'd be able to get up on mornings like this one and go for a run or go shopping or get a makeover and come home wearing lots of sexy smoky black eyeliner. And I wouldn't care when he made comments about how women were prettier without makeup, because I'd know *that* was a lie, a truth he could not hold dear. The eyeliner in fact would make him want to fuck my lights out, and I'd let him, and then I'd fall asleep while maybe *he* stayed awake to worry, for a change, remembering that I was the young tender, here. That *I* was the catch. But I loved him. And the thought of being without him—I couldn't even endure it. When I thought of my life without him, the winds swept over, and there wasn't a green leaf anywhere. Empty, empty. And now I could keep after him to admit he did something pointless and horny and lowlife and gross, or I could stomp out the tiny pissed-off-ness in my heart and cut my losses and move on.

"I'm sorry," I said. "I'm sorry I made you go. This is all my fault. I'm sorry I misinterpreted your behavior. I'm sorry I made it into something else. I'm sorry."

And Ian came to me, and held me against his skinny chest while I cried.

We went along for a few days, trying to act like everything was okay, and then one night we had a perfectly lovely time and I fell asleep afterward, and woke up because he was no longer in bed beside me. I found him on the computer and sidled up behind him. He hit the back button just before I saw her picture.

"What's up?" he said, and swiveled his chair around to look at me.

"What's up in *here?*" I leaned over him and tapped on a link and there was a picture of Luna, naked on all fours. "I knew it. I *knew* it!"

"Knew what?" Ian said. He was expansive, tipped back in his chair. "It's true, she sent me a link to her Web site. I knew you would resent our friendship and so I didn't bring it up."

"Your *friendship?*" All I ever did anymore was repeat after him.

"Yes, our friendship."

"Those are nude pictures of her!"

"She had her clothes off in these pictures. That is true. She wanted me to look at her Web site and give her an opinion of her photographs."

"Let me guess. To you they're just mammary glands."

"You would do this," Ian said. "I hadn't even thought about that until you brought it up. Leave it to you. When I see these pictures, I practically don't even notice. That she has her shirt off. It's true, to me they are mammary glands. That's what they're for. They're meant to suckle young, not to be seen as something sick, as something twisted and *sexual*."

"Oh *really?*"

"Don't you dare," Ian said.

But I went for it anyway. I gave him a little pop quiz and touched his crotch. "I knew it. Exactly. That's how much you think of them as mammary glands."

"Do you know that there is something very wrong with you?"

"With me? With *me?*" I wanted to grab my hair at the roots and run shrieking out onto the street going *cuckoo! Cuckoo! I'm cuckoo for Cocoa Puffs!*

"I need to get my mat before I totally freak out."

"Ooh, I'm so scared. Not the mat, please don't get the mat!"

Ian slapped me across the face. "You do this," he said, his voice shaking. "You do this to me. To yourself. You push me and push me and make me do things."

"This is not my fault!"

"Of course it's your fault. You're pathetic and jealous and I swore to myself I'd never put up with some jealous possessive girlfriend who thinks she owns me."

"You know what, Ian? You are more fucked up than I realized."

"You come in here, you intrude on my privacy and accuse me of ridiculous things. Just like your mom did with Allen. Always trying to control him."

"Fuck you."

This time he shoved me, but Ian wasn't exactly the hugest boyfriend on the planet. I shoved him back a whole lot harder and he stumbled into the bookcase, bringing down several books and his Windhorse prayer flag, which is supposed to be increasing his Lung-ta, or giving him good energy or whatever.

Lung-ta, ha ha.

Ian shrieked and snatched the flag before it hit the ground/me. I guess it was like any flag, sacred. It killed me. His little girly shriek and that his flag was what he cared about.

"Mister Buddhist man," I said. "Mister Buddhist man wife-beater." I was crying, but I knew a few things. I knew about the three marks of existence. I know that they're impermanence, suffering, and no-self.

Which pretty much summed up Ian and me, emphasis on the first mark.

In my next life, I plan to be a woman who doesn't get told

all the time by some pseudo-Buddhist fuck of a boyfriend that everything is all her fault. I plan to be a woman who won't even remotely fall in love with the guy. I plan not to be looking up at him from my vantage point on the floor, wondering where we go from here and knowing already that it will take more, even, than this before I call it quits. Tomorrow I'll be applying concealer to the bruise on my cheek and Ian will scold me, though playfully, for the green bruise on his shin. This wasn't my life, I was thinking. This is some other woman's life.

But Ian was crying. Possibly he was thinking something along these same lines.

We did better than a lot of couples I know. We weren't saddled with kids and we both liked our jobs and when we did get along, we got along great. Ian made me laugh and he didn't expect me to clean the house all the time. We liked to go out drinking and spend time with friends and hike and go out to breakfast late on the weekends, treating our hangovers with greasy eggs and bacon. Except for times like this, we had a sweet life.

Ian was curled in a ball next to me and I touched his shoulder. We were both sorry. And one fact was indisputable: if I hadn't dragged him to American Bush, none of this would've happened. He was right. I started it.

In my next life, I plan to be a woman so stunning that he'll never want to look at a single other woman ever again. I plan to have tons of self-confidence and drive a small white sports car fast around corners and indulge myself with luxury items like real crystal champagne flutes and velvet sofas. I plan to have kids. I plan to live in the suburbs and make it look both subversive and desirable. I stroked Ian's hair, imagining it.

The
Apology

THE COME-ON-AND-GO-Hawaiian Benefit Bash was to take place on Friday night, in the auditorium of the preschool.

And for weeks now, Rose had been hard at work. She was the chairperson; and there were parents who took such roles seriously and those who didn't, and Rose was one of the serious ones. There were other parents, mothers mostly, who were assigned such roles and then acted like slobs, letting their machine take messages, and missing meetings and not writing things on the schedule whatsoever, not *planning*, the way such an event needed really and for months ahead of time to be planned. These were the mothers who let their children's teeth rot because they were too distracted to make dental appointments; and they let things fall to other, more put-together women like Rose, who really wasn't more put-together at all, but frankly driven (as *all* parents should be, she thought) by simple guilt and duty. Did they think she liked getting up earlier than the rest? Did they think she just *naturally* remembered that a certain Thursday was Orange Day at the preschool, and so made a note to herself to dress Max in his rust-colored coveralls and Georgie in an orange T-shirt and peach-colored pants? The point was: *orange*. It wasn't the hardest thing in the world to remember. It was what the good mothers of the world *did*. This she believed. And did those other mothers, the ones who blew off or laughed off Orange Day, think she liked attending lengthy meetings in which often practically nothing was accomplished, or spending hours on end shopping for tiki torches and grass skirts for the preschool faculty? It wasn't *fun* work; she didn't do these things because she enjoyed them. She did them because it was her job; just as her job, before children, had been working as a paralegal in an attorney's office.

And because motherhood and wifehood was the sort of job where there were few deadlines, finally, and where having the self-discipline—to keep up with getting dressed and out of the house every morning for fresh air, and getting the car inspected and buying groceries and a million other menial tasks—was so very important, Rose had long ago devised for herself a private system involving her ProForm LX treadmill, which she used each and every morning without fail. Depending on the trans- gression (a PTA meeting forgotten; a phone call, or a library book, unreturned; a milk ticket absent from one of the boys' lunchbox), she added a .5 mile sprint to her morning workout. It was a small thing. It burned almost one hundred extra calories! It took only a few extra minutes, and left her panting and absolved.

And if you didn't treat a life that way—if she didn't rise each and every morning with determination and a checklist and consequences for sloth—you were bound, she was bound, to lapse into depression, and to feel trivial and female. That was Rose's thinking. You got up in the morning and you did things in the world because, as a housewife, there weren't a whole lot of other options.

Anyway, that was the way she presented it to her husband, Kevin. Because he thought she did it too much—volunteered.

You had to present it that way: as work. Anyone would. Because if it was not work, it was *pleasure*. And if it was pleasure that being the chairperson for the Come-On-and-Go-Hawaiian Benefit Bash gave her, then that meant her interests were small and immediate, as easy as making phone calls and collecting donations—which really wasn't easy at all, considering the mothers who were forever forgetting their checkbooks or refusing to pick up the phone. Yet people saw it that way, Rose reflected bitterly. And thought that she was a silly mother goose. And she couldn't explain, not to anyone ever, that it was exactly the smallness of such events that moved her. Exactly the fact that the events came and went, year in and year out, settling like beads on a cord, making for the children and teachers and parents these, the very very happiest of years: when the children were small.

People—like Kevin—jokingly called her a Martha Stewart, meaning of course a control freak. (He would miss the Benefit Bash, if he could. He would see the leis, and chortle, and refuse to get in the spirit of things. He would see the coconut-shaped tumblers and wonder what they had cost, and ask what was the point of a Hawaiian theme party in January? What was the point of a Hawaiian theme party, *ever?*) Perhaps, he'd suggested, that was precisely why she'd volunteered to be the chairperson, way back in August. To have something to do and worry over.

But that wasn't it.

She did these things—she *did*—out of love.

Every day for four years now, she'd brought Max and Georgie to this building. It smelled like pencils and glue and industrial-strength floor shine and tramped-in snow on winter days. And upstairs was the small administrative office where, daily, women gathered as though at a kitchen table, to talk about children and to swap war stories about the husbands. And the hallway with its coat pegs, and the bathrooms further down with their tiny toilets and sinks. And every day in the hallway, on the stairwell, was the hubbub of so many small and happy and busy lives: the art projects to collect, and the coats and bags, and the adults trying to get a word in edge-wise and tuition checks being dropped off in the office, and the book-order money, and the daily spectacle of happy tired kids traipsing in from the playground. They filed past the waiting parents, looking shyly for their own.

And all this, all this, Rose treasured. The children would not always be little. And then all this would go away. And so she'd meant for her work as chairperson to be a sort of finale, a gift offered up from her humble mother's heart.

Two days before the event, Rose drove around the valley col-lecting items for the silent auction. There were over fifty donations, ranging from a gift certificate for BOTOX treatment to a weekend in Sun Valley to cheese-and-cracker gift bas-kets. She delivered them to the preschool and took a look around the auditorium. The tables would go on this end, and the food in the hallway, so that people could move past the auction items in the foyer upstairs, then get a plate, file past the beverage bar, get their food, and head for the dining tables. And how would she get the tiki lamps to stand up? But there were committees and subcommittees. Other people helping. She reminded herself that she would remember, above all things, to be a gracious host. It would be a disaster if she was speeding around and wound-up and anxious. The previous year, she and Kevin had attended a party where the hostess zoomed around setting out napkins and plates, then dragged the scrabbling dog across the kitchen floor, shutting it in the garage before the doorbell rang again. "How are you doing?" Rose had asked stupidly. "I'll be *fine*, once *this* whole goddamn fucking thing is over," the hostess had said.

Rose tried to keep this in mind, even when the caterer, Rodney, called to confirm the number of guests as forty, instead of *four hundred.*

"You did say forty," Rodney said.

"No. I wouldn't have." Rose said. She panicked, dug for her list.

"Well, that's what I have written here."

"I know perfectly well that there are several *hundred* people who'll be attending. I have the list right in front of me."

"Okay. All right. Have it your way. That's just a whole mess of pineapple kabobs more," he said.

"Yes, it is. Can you handle it?"

"Handle it! I've done weddings with up to a thousand people."

"Thank God. That's right, it's right here. Three hundred and seventeen people have already RSVP'd."

"Have it your way," Rodney said. Rose could hear the smile in his voice. It was not her mistake; it was almost never her mistake. All the same, she hung up the phone and changed into her running clothes. She added the half-mile sprint to her workout, thinking about the way the gymnasium had looked the evening before. She'd gone to look the place over and to decide where to put the items for the silent auction. An AA meeting had just adjourned. She knew the room was a public space, and she did not mean to be hard-hearted. Still. Would it kill them to clear out their literature and coffee cups? Then there was Rodney. How could he have thought she'd said *forty?*

Rose hooked herself to the treadmill, and cranked the speed.

And then it was the day of the party.

Rose set her alarm for five-thirty in the morning. She got up and made herself toast and coffee and then embarked on the day. There were more errands to run (real coconuts, for decoration; the party store yet again, for more paper tablecloths; the rental place, to add an additional forty chairs to the list; and the bank, to deposit the check from the preschool; and two more items that had come in for the silent auction; and ice for the coolers), and she rushed through them, and tripped over curbs and turned on the windshield wipers in her car several times accidentally and left her sunglasses somewhere and her list somewhere else, and so had to backtrack. And still it grew closer and closer to evening, and still there seemed to be loose ends, and she arrived at the auditorium an hour-and-a-half early, which as it happened was not nearly, nearly early enough.

One of the dads had brought oil for the tiki lamps. It was a last-minute item Rose had decided to delegate to Karl, whose son was in the same preschool class as Max.

"I hope there's enough," Karl said, and set down the box. He unloaded eight large jugs. "Do you want me to get started filling them?"

"That's citronella oil," Rose said.

"What?"

"It's citronella."

"Crap!" Karl said. "Crap! Oh, man. Man, I am so sorry."

"We can't burn that in here. We'll asphyxiate everybody."

"Yeah. That would be ugly. Wait, I'm gonna call Lowe's. I didn't even notice. He just took me to the aisle and I loaded up. I kind of left this errand to the last minute is what I think happened."

Rose found a quiet corner and called Kevin. "You have to find something!" she told him. "I just want to kill him."

"Well, he meant well."

"I know. Of course he meant well. He meant well, only now one of the very main and most important features of a party, the *lighting*, is going to be ruined. Please, please find oil. We can't keep these overheads on. It looks like an AA meeting in here." She was close to tears, and she pulled the deep pink lily from behind her ear and fingered the petals. Her fingers shook. "I can't believe it. Here I've been working for weeks, and I ask someone else to do this one, one thing, and now look."

"It's going to be okay."

"I know," Rose said. But still her hands trembled, and still she felt that this one small bad thing could not help but lead to others, and then others. The point was to keep that first thread from unraveling; that was the only way to live a life. And yet the only way to do this was to count on other people, who would fail her, like now. "How can it look like Hawaii without the tiki torches?" she said. Her voice caught. She saw a ukulele player step up to the mike, tap it, and frown. "And people are already getting here."

"It's going to be a good night no matter what," Kevin said. "With or without the torches. Go stand in a corner and say the Serenity prayer."

• • •

The auction, at least, went smoothly. The parents and teachers, most all sporting the suggested Hawaiian attire, had joked and bidded and bantered and raised over two thousand dollars for the preschool. But it was bright; so bright! And people were dragging chairs around, and laughing too loud and talking too loud. Meanwhile the director of the preschool, Alison, stood onstage in a white sweater; stood before the microphone with her mouth moving. Someone tried again plugging and unplugging it, but it was no use, and Rose moved toward the stage. They'd tested the microphone hours earlier; it was pure comedy, if it wouldn't work now.

Alison waited a few minutes, then tapped the mike, smiled and shrugged. Two more volunteers, other mothers, were milling around Rose, asking questions: Where was the Audiovisual room? Did they have another microphone? *Welcome*, Alison said finally, trying to project her voice, *welcome to the Fifteenth Annual Benefit Bash, thank you so much—*.

Then another wave of sound, so that Rose felt compelled to act. Everyone happy and drinking and silverware and glasses clanking. The brightness.

Rose took matters into her own hands. She stood. She had intended only an announcement, but it was too noisy for that—it would have to be a yell.

So she yelled it, trying to sound sporting: "Please be quiet!" She smiled out at the crowd and brought a finger to her lips. Were they idiots? Didn't they know better? Alison, the director of the very preschool they had gathered on *this very night* to honor, was *trying to be heard.*

This did nothing. She felt sickness and heat in her throat at the thought of Alison's being drowned out. It was *important.* Alison's speech, her own words of thanks, important. Rose waited a few minutes, and still Alison went on soundlessly. Then something came up in her and Rose moved closer to the stage, thinking *rescue*, thinking *stop*, thinking *help*. "Be quiet!" Rose shouted again, and still no one seemed to hear, and all around her was disaster, the guests loud and tipsy and no one listening, no one at all.

And what Rose could not reconcile, above all things, was her love for this world and what had happened next. She tried so *hard* to be good; she tried so hard to give herself and her husband, and above all her sons, the kind of life they would all remember and treasure. She'd invested whole years of her life in this work. It was not small. It was not pointless. It mattered. She got out of bed each and every day, and shouldered up her life, and did things, *did* things, the errands, the phone calls, the gym, the dentists. She set goals, and met them. She sent thank-you notes, answered her e-mail, and all this finally with the expectation that eventually she might see the fruits of her labor: to have, for example, the house the neighborhood kids would want to come to, to be the neighbor on the street you could ask favors of, and also she wanted to be kind, and remembered as kind, because she *was* all that—a good person.

Except for when she had these—these *moments*—of leakage, for lack of a better word. Where her real self came out. Spectacularly, awesomely. She would think of it later with her mouth ajar, and she would weep, knowing this was how they would remember her.

Because the third time, into the brightness, into the noise, Rose had yelled something else.

"Shut the *fuck up!*" she'd cried.

Loud!

And at last, the guests were quiet.

She saw their puzzled sad faces turned to her, the faces of people she cared for. Friends. And she had meant well, and also meant for it maybe to come out sounding funny, as in another group of friends—admittedly, it was a stretch—it may have come out sounding funny. She had meant to—oh, she had meant to *help* Alison, to protect her, to somehow defend her honor. She had meant to show—well—*reverence* for this world, all of it so much a part of the world she loved.

Alison paused, then began to speak again. This time hers was the only voice. She stood sweetly in white, thanking everyone, meaning it. She even thanked Rose.

And at long last, once the band resumed playing, Rose made a break for it. She slithered out, skulked out, though really this was not much possible in the too-loud, too-bright room.

A mother, Rose discovered over the weekend, did not necessarily have to get out of bed.

The first day, she changed from her pajamas into her exercise clothes. But there weren't enough miles in the world to sprint; she'd fall over dead first. Rose crawled back under the covers and cried herself to sleep.

The next day, she let Kevin take Max and Georgie to the zoo and the arcade and to the movies and to return videos and finally, to do the grocery shopping. Rose lay in bed, crying and thinking and imagining the scene of her outburst over and over again.

At last she called her best friend, Linda.

"What are you, Catholic?" Linda said. "Quit beating yourself up! It's a funny story!"

"I can't," Rose said. "I can't. I yelled it in front of five hundred people. These are people I've cared about for years. I can't get over it. I can't get over it."

"What would it take for you to feel better?"

"A time machine. Self-mutilation."

"Oh, please. By Monday everyone will have forgotten."

But Rose thought, well, but there should be a place to put this grief. There should be a grill I can whisper into, and a hard wooden seat.

Rose lived, mostly, in a world without faith. She did not believe in God. And so she drove around sometimes, bereft, wanting to give things away: money, or food, or tenderness. She had too much of everything, and most of their friends had too much of everything, and it felt exactly like rushing around with a beautiful newborn in her arms. And wanting to say to the gods, and to the circling crows and the dark sky, *oh you wouldn't want this baby, not this one, this one is crippled and ugly, and pockmarked and frail and useless*. But still the birds dipped and flapped, closing in.

By the third day, a Sunday, Rose had transitioned into a calm that led to what she thought were fairly profound musings on her own life. She blew her nose and folded her hands on the bedspread and stared out the window.

Until this point, she thought, until this *incident*—hers had been a pitiful existence. She'd lived each day in fear that this lovely world would get taken away. Every day she'd worried. Every day she'd been afraid, of big things and small. And so she'd structured her life accordingly: with rules and responsibilities, and consequences for days badly lived, punishments for mistakes made. That was the only way to stay happy: to feel that there were clear rules, and even clearer outcomes. And yet all her effort, all her days of planning and shopping in anticipation of the Benefit Bash, had come to a single moment: the moment when she'd lost control and opened her big fat mouth and yelled that thing.

And on some level it made *sense* that she had done it. Risked her good life. Her happiness had always felt provisional, something that could be snatched from her in a second. She had too much; too much good luck. Even her children, even when they drove her crazy, seemed too beautiful, too unlikely. And so she had tried, tried daily. To keep all the balls in the air. To keep her happiness.

And then, to have yelled what she'd yelled over the heads of so many parents, so many friends, and undo everything— that was how it felt. That even as her daily efforts accrued— hurrah, she'd remembered his jacket and mittens thirty days in a row!—even as she was getting credit for these things, she could with absolutely no warning whatsoever make such an ass of herself. And offend people she cared for, and it was this— this leakage, of her angry and unruly self, at dinner, that she could not bear. That's what had gotten her to this point, puffy-faced and bedridden, being offered canned soup and stale oyster crackers. That was why she'd ruined it, the Come-On-and-Go-Hawaiian Benefit Bash, by yelling *shut the fuck up!* at everybody, meaning well, sure—didn't we *all*—but leveling her success with that single, memorably worded eruption.

As though—after all—her whole happy life might be exactly as provisional as she'd suspected.

She woke in the night to reach for Kevin.

"I'm suffering," she said.

"I know you are, sweetie," he said, and took her hand.

"I'm *suffering*. I meant well. I can't believe I would do such a thing, I can't believe I would do such a thing, there are moms who are never going to speak to me probably ever again, kids who won't be able to come play, because I said it. I hate myself."

"It's okay. It's going to be okay. Don't beat yourself up too much. It's probably already been forgotten."

Her husband was kind. He was never anything but kind. He knew about self-love; he rarely beat himself up over things. When they went to dinner, afterward he'd repeat to his wife all the funny things he'd said at the table. She was the opposite. She was all about humiliation and self-hate.

And what was the point of that?

"Thank you for giving me so much help this weekend," Rose said. "Thank you for not making me get up. I'm going to tell everyone I'm sorry tomorrow. At the preschool."

Kevin had no guilt. He'd fallen back asleep. Rose slipped out of bed and put on her running shoes. Then she went to the family room and lowered the treadmill ramp to the floor. But it was no good. She stepped on the thing, then off again, and went back upstairs to bed.

It had not been forgotten.

Rose went into the building, and started to cry and went back out to the car again, and then finally back inside. But when she spoke the tears came, and she couldn't make them stop, and it was worse that all three women in the office did not even have to ask why she was crying, and in this way, Rose was given to understand that her outburst had been the topic of at least one or two conversations. She could not hold her head stupidly up. She could not be cavalier. What she had said and done in front of everyone *mattered*. And maybe it was true, that the thing she'd said was sort of funny; and maybe it was true, that it was what everyone else had *wanted* to yell that night at the dinner. But still she hated herself, and needed to cry against them, and needed to believe she still had a place here.

And there was love in the air. They were not holding a grudge. Alison hugged her and forgave her. Sally, too. It was a lovely day, with green everywhere and an occasional gust of wind that made her feel just a bit lighter, and Rose spent a few quiet minutes on the playground. Soon enough it would all be gone, the parents and the playground and the chatter over paper plates at preschool dinners. And the coats and colored maps, too, the hallways quiet, the parking lot empty. She had said a stupid thing: that was all.

She pumped herself on one of the small swings, and tried to work up a few jokes to sustain her for the next little while:

Actually, I suffer from Tourette.

Hey, way to invite Linda Blair to the Benefit Bash!

And: *Excuse me, but I'm off to my anger management class.*

"How was it?" Kevin asked.

"I'm so lucky. I'm so lucky. I love that school, I love that place. Forgiveness rained from the heavens."

"Was it okay?" He held her. She liked that they were nearly the same size, and that she could look over his shoulder when he took her in his arms like this. It was pleasant, his bony frame and the way she could rest her chin.

"They were great," she said. "They were *amazing*. It felt like Jesus."

"Oh, good. I'm sorry. You try so *hard*."

"I really do. I didn't mean to screw things up."

"You were memorable, anyway. More like a rock star than a mother, is how you should think of it. Maybe next year you can smash up an electric guitar."

"Except that there won't be a next year, thank goodness," Rose said. She would never be more than what she was: a good mother, and one who could do no more than to try to practice, daily, the small tasks of a good life, even if it meant flubbing them. Rose thought of the way some of the people had looked at her that night in the auditorium, their confusion and sorrow so plain. *I thought we were friends*, their faces seemed to say. And, *what's wrong, what's so terribly wrong inside?* But whatever it was, Rose could not put into words.

Hangman

SO. POSSIBLY, HIS WIFE was pregnant.

When he heard this, Owen couldn't help but blurt out a few useful questions. Was it too late for the morning-after pill? (Yes.) Did she hate him for asking? (Of course.)

It wasn't as if she'd tricked him, exactly. With the other two children downstairs watching *Teletubbies*, he'd allowed Sara to straddle him lovingly on the toilet seat. He'd forgotten himself. He'd believed the counting she did aloud, backward from the day of her last period or forward from the day of her last cycle or whatever it was, but it was busy and steamy there in the after-bath, and whatever.

That was how it had happened, or possibly happened.

Owen went to the window and looked out at all the crunchy gray. It was February, and there were no surprises. There were the gray tree limbs and straggly lilac bushes and pebbles beneath the swing set, and the weathered cedar fence and the side of the garage, still streaked with pink from an entire box of strawberry milkshake-flavored Go-GURTS that the boys had stomped on months ago, sure they'd lost TV privileges for three days but that made no difference to anyone because the pink mess was still there and probably always would be, part of the scenery. He went to the bureau and dug out fresh socks and boxers. "Jesus," he said. "I hope you're not knocked up. I don't know where we'd find the energy for a third. I'm tired all the time *now*."

Her retort, from the bed, was swift and heated and sharp. For starters, she was too old, she pointed out, to be referred to as "knocked up." She told him so.

Though, really, it came out more like this: *It's aggressive and adolescent and posturing and violent-sounding and it makes the guy sound self-important, like he's done it all, like he gets the credit, like he's done some great violent thing to the woman and well guess what I just totally hate it. And if you go to work this morning, and if you go around broadcasting all over the office that you've done this thing to me, well I will just kick your ass seriously. And the worst part is that I can't even believe you'd bring up RU 483 or RU 486 or whatever it is since you know I just totally, totally just really really with all my heart, so that I'm walking around bawling all the time, want another baby.*

Patiently, Owen smoothed and folded his pajama pants before depositing them in the drawer. At most, if she was actually knocked—oops, pregnant—she was a week in; yet already her body seemed to be heating at night, a remarkably compressed and clay-like heat that made sleeping next to her nearly impossible. A green malaria heat, a pissed-off cover-kicking heat.

And that was just *nighttime*.

Because, *if* she was pregnant, in the daytime would be—he'd lived through it twice now—the furious tornado-housecleaning wife, the shooter of flinty-eyed looks and the taker of potshots by a woman enduring her first trimester. Then she was predatory and unfamiliar, creeping up from behind to hiss criticisms, and waking him at night to pick fights, and seeming to hate him with every ounce of energy and from the bottom of her hormone-logged heart. He crept around the house, meek and trying to help but mostly just frightened—she was like a grenade with the pin pulled out—and this was blessed fertility, this was his earth goddess.

And he thought now, in his dark heart, that if she really *were* knocked up, or blessed with child or whatever you wanted to call it—well, then, Owen realized that they were more or less just totally fucked.

The point was, if she was pregnant, he knew better than to argue. He had seen her pregnant before! So he paused; and then, idiot that he apparently still was, waded into the crocodile-infested waters with pythons twisting in the branches over-head. And said politely, "I just like it that 'knocked up' sounds irreverent."

"It sounds hateful, is what it sounds. I'm sorry, I shouldn't have gone off, I should keep my mouth shut, I know you hate the thought of another baby even though I totally really want another one and I can't even believe you'd ask. About the morning-after pill. Because I'm too old for that one too, we both are if you ask me, I'm not saying it would be easy because in a lot of ways it would suck but I'm seriously so baby-hungry again, I can't help it. I can't help it. And I'm afraid to even take the blood test. Which, I'd get an accurate result even if I went in and did it today, but I'm afraid to take it because I want another baby *so bad* and I swear if I go in for the test it will come out negative and then I'll get my heart broken because the only way I'll ever be able to have another baby is if it happens like this, if it's an accident, and I know how much you hate the thought and I'm probably not pregnant anyway. So I'm sorry I jumped on you. But it does, it sounds *terrible*—knocked up! Like you Tarzan, me Jane."

"That's not what I think," he said. "You know that. That's not what I mean when I say it."

"Well, then what do you? Mean? Why don't you put it another way? How about, 'My wife's pregnant?'"

"Might be pregnant."

"Whatever!"

"I just like the irreverence. That's all. It doesn't sound so holy."

"Doesn't sound so holy? Doesn't sound so *holy?*" she was thrashing her way out from under the sheets.

"I just mean it to be funny," he said. "Is all." He had twenty minutes to get ready for work and yet there she was, crouched and coiled and furious on her side of the bed, and really there was just no way to get from his spot in front of the bureau to the bedroom door.

"Well it's not."

"Well then, okay."

"I'm just saying, rise above. That you're too old for it. That you don't need to go around saying, knocked up."

"Jesus, okay. Okay!"

"Okay is right."

She was looking all around the room for something to pick a fight about. But he'd picked up his clothes; and made, as always and diplomatically and something he had done all the years of their marriage, his own side of the bed.

"You don't have to be irreverent. You're more wonderful when you're *not*. That doesn't make you dull."

"I can't even express how sorry I am that I ever said it."

"You have to promise me you won't talk about it at work. You have to promise me, until I know for sure."

"Okay, okay, okay."

"And I do," she said. "Hope I am."

He called her from work. He could hear both boys shrieking in the background. "Maybe we can talk about it more when I get home tonight," Owen said.

"Are you calling me from the john? You'd better not be calling me from the john. I hate that so much!"

"This is the only time I had!" Owen said.

"I never want to talk about it anymore with you ever again," Sara replied. "If I am, I am. And I'm probably not. But at least, for the next week and because I feel so weird, I really want to be able to at least pretend I am. Okay? And then I'll probably just get my period and you'll be off the hook. But in the meantime we at least won't have any more fights. Okay?"

He tried to imagine how it would be. Their two boys—well, they were great. And growing up, and old enough finally to do things like play Go Fish and watch movies with human characters rather than just cartoons. They had, Owen thought, a hard but very nice life—overall. They had conversations and symmetry. Best of all, he and Sara seemed to be coming out of the long dark smothering tunnel of worry worry worry, all the small worries of having very small children, the anxiety of stairs and choking hazards and speeding cars and household cleaners under the sink. They were going on dates again, and actually having sex once in a while, and planning the occasional weekend getaway and so on.

Three kids—he could scarcely imagine it! Three kids spelled trouble. Three kids meant not just another carseat, and that whole thing of going from infant back-facing to infant front-facing to toddler seat to booster seat and all that, but probably another *car*—something like, well, a minivan— and probably even another *house*, really.

What could she be thinking? To want another?

Here was a good conversation they had over and over. Always like this:

Him: *How can you want another baby, when you see how hard our lives are now? When you see what babies lead to? The kids are so great, but they wear us out.*

Her: *How can you want to have sex all the time, when you see what it leads to? Same thing, right? It's just biology. For both of us.*

They had this conversation about three times a week.

The next week passed happily. Sara hummed and got busy organizing and even had the nerve to haul home a pair of brand-new tiny black Converse sneakers. She was gearing up—clearly—exercising and popping vitamins and maintaining an uncharacteristically cheerful disposition. She devoted the weekend to repainting the boys' bedroom and didn't ask for Owen's help. She appreciated Owen's manhood several nights in a row (fine with him; she could fiddle with the hose without getting near the faucet), and wore thin bright frocks while working in the garden and also did something new to her hair and nestled close to him at night. In between, he drove sadly to and from work, and tried to imagine buying plane tickets not just for a family of four but *five*, and thought about how it was all very well and good that she wanted another child except that she didn't seem to, not really; which was to say that she let him each and every night put both kids to bed without her assistance, and apparently saw no wrong in this, and wanted maybe perhaps another *baby* but not exactly another *child*. And so Owen kept a flask of tequila behind his computer monitor to sip mournfully every night after she and the boys had gone off to bed.

Then her period started, and then the tears. Sara cried, she beseeched, she took long walks at night and now, damned if every time they went out in public together they didn't see babies everywhere fresh from the oven and gorgeous and plump-limbed, so that now and again even Owen would feel his own heart go buttery. But babies were one thing and children were another. He held firm, and this in spite of the fact that now they were *all* in cahoots: Sara, Toby, and Paul.

"I'll give you one hundred dollars," she told Toby one night at dinner, "if you can talk daddy into letting us have another baby."

"A hundred dollars?" Toby said. "For reals?"

"For reals."

"You don't have that much money!"

"Sure I do," Sara said, and smiled at Owen. "A hundred bucks. I'll give you a hundred bucks in *ones*."

"No way!"

"Yes way," Sara said, and smiled sweetly at Paul. "Wouldn't you like to have a new baby in the house?" Paul was three and tender, a lover of animals small.

"Yes, I would!" Paul cried.

"Stop," Owen said. "Please, act your age."

"I can't," Sara said. "I really can't. I've tried. I'm sorry. I'm going to call her Lily."

When again a few weeks later she reached for him, gently he reached for his own equipment in the nightstand drawer; and they went on like this, and at least her fury and heat had passed, at least until the next hormonal surge or ebb; and he was only a little nervous, wondering at her silence.

At most, he concluded, her baby hunger would mean another pet. Since the last close call, Owen actually felt *down* with the almost certainly impending trip to the pet store. As it was, they had two parakeets and a turtle and a fish tank and a Shih-Tzu. As it was, the Shih-Tzu was herself menstruating, leaving small brownish-pink stains on the couch and in her dog bed. If anything was going to provoke her, Owen thought, it was that; but Sara hummed and smiled, smiled and hummed, squirting the stains with Resolve carpet cleaner and making not even the slightest fuss. It was creepy, but he allowed himself to relax a little. She couldn't make him. He would let her act like a child, if it made her feel better. He'd let her eggs go on dropping. There would be no help from him.

She brought it up again a few nights later.

"We can have sex *every single night for a year*. If you'll just think about it. If you'll even just consider it."

"Baloney. You'll welch," Owen said. "You already destroyed your credibility with that puppy thing."

"That was a puppy. I'm talking about a human baby. I kid you not, if you even tell me you'll just think about it, just open the topic for consideration, I will. Through my period, through illness and yeast infections and whatever else. Swear to god."

"Like you kept the promise with the puppy?"

"That's not fair!" Sara said.

The puppy thing was two years ago. She'd called him three times in four hours; hours, he learned later, when she'd stood before the same cage of puppies at the pound.

"I do not want another dog," was what he'd said in the first conversation.

"I know you don't technically want one, but what does that mean?"

"That means, I don't want another dog."

"On a scale of one to ten, how mad would you be?"

"Eleven," Owen said.

"This is killing me," she said in the next call, an hour later. "I really want another baby. I want another human baby. But this would be okay. I'd settle for this. For another dog. Because, you know, small dogs always seem like babies, even after they've grown up, because they're not as smart as big dogs, at least I've never had a smart small dog, and they always just stay looking little. And cute."

"Pause the game," he told Toby. And to Sara, "I can't even believe this. We have enough stuff going on!"

"She's tiny," Sara said. "I think she might be part beagle. And I kid you not, when I hold her against my chest I swear I'm about to start lactating. She's so tiny. She's so *needy*. This is killing me! I really want her!"

"Beagles are awful, awful dogs," he said.

"Please?"

"I'm not your dad. I'm not going to give you permission. I don't want another dog. I told you that. If you bring it home,

I'll be mad. You asked. I'm telling you. You'll bring it home, and you'll expect me to help. You'll bring it home and next thing you know I'll be scooping up poop in the yard."

"I'm the one who cleans up the yard now. I'm the one who does all of the yard work!"

"Then you'll be expecting me to let it out at night when it barks. Or whatever."

"Owen, I'll do anything. I really want her."

"Toby wants to get back to the game."

"Can't you just consider it?"

"Sure, I'll consider it. Hmmm, let me think: no."

She laid down her chips with the third call. "They're about to close," she said. "I'll make you a deal."

It was getting dark, and Owen was ready to have her home. "Sara, don't do this. You're making me feel like the big bad-ass husband. I'm sorry, I know you want that thing, but it would suck. You know it would. We already have too much going on."

"You don't want to barter even remotely?"

"Like what?"

"If you let me bring her home, I'll give you ten blow jobs."

"No."

"Okay, thirty."

"You'll give me thirty blow jobs if I say yes to the puppy? Thirty consecutively, or like spread out over a year or what?" He'd believe it when he saw it.

"Not consecutive," Sara said. "What do I, look like Rod Stewart?"

"You won't really do it."

"I will. I swear to god. One a night for a month if you want."

"And you'll really really do it? And you won't make me

help take care of it? You won't cajole me into taking it for walks or anything?"

"I swear."

"What is that thing?" Owen said, when she brought it home. "Is that its real hair?"

"Singin' a different tune now, aren't ya?" Sara said. "I'm sorry I had to stoop that low. Blow jobs should be free for you. But thank you. I love her. I love her! Thank you!" she kissed him. The boys were playing with the kid across the street, and so Owen cornered her and rubbed himself against her. "Can I cash in one of my coupons right now?"

"Right this second?" Sara said. "We just walked in. I at least have to make her a bed. And think up a name. I think I'm going to name her Olive. What do you think?"

He followed Sara to the bathroom, where she pulled a clean sweatshirt from the dryer and made a bed and put the puppy on top. It was all white except for a lemony patch over one eye. It trembled and looked briefly at Owen, then sighed and settled into a ball.

Sara made good.

The next day the puppy crapped all over and howled when they left it alone for even one minute. Sara had to carry it around all the time. She broke out the fabric sling she'd used to carry the boys when they were infants, but the puppy slipped out and hit the floor. But the boys went to their grandmother's for dinner, and so Sara ponied up again, and Owen fell asleep afterward.

• • •

It wasn't like a normal puppy, and that was because—as Owen had tried to caution her—the thing was part beagle. Normal puppies yipped and cried, but Olive carried on like a gibbon at daybreak. And she had issues with anger. When reprimanded, Olive snapped and more than once broke skin and didn't much seem to realize that *she* was the *dog*. That she was the one without civil rights.

They were into the second week, and Sara's enthusiasm was flagging. Once she mentioned TMJ and rubbed at her jaw, but Owen was pitiless and anyway had in fact already had to let the puppy out twice now, and had already had to get rid of his one remaining sneaker. He counted; he had twenty-one jobs left. He took his pleasure, and felt only a little bad when she said, after, listening to the keening downstairs, "I wish I'd never brought that thing home."

The puppy lasted another three days. Then Sara placed an ad, and said what they sometimes said to one another, a phrase that worked beautifully in a marriage, which was this:

She said, "Let us never speak of it again."

Then they shook on it.

"No way!" she said, when he inquired about job number nineteen. "You've had your fun."

"Are you kidding?" There was a bulge in his boxers. He'd gotten himself all excited just anticipating it. And now here they were.

"I got rid of the thing!"

"Since when was that a contingency?"

"Well," she said. She was propped up in bed, filing her nails. "Did you keep your receipt?"

And that was the puppy thing.

But that had been two years ago. Now and again, it irked Owen to think of the unpaid bill, the eleven ecstasies she'd denied him. But that wasn't quite right; he'd had blow jobs since. Plenty! But those hadn't been *payment*; those hadn't been the ones she'd promised, his little Indian giver, and no matter how he thought of it they'd always be out there somewhere in the universe, free-floating, unborn.

"Sure, we can have sex every night for a year," Owen said now. "Fine with me."

"You won't even think about it, though, will you?" Sara's voice broke. "You won't. You won't ever. Have another baby with me."

"No," Owen said. "I can't. I can't. I swear to you, I swear to you, we'd wind up getting divorced. I just don't have it in me. I'm sorry."

Sara cried for a while, then kissed the boys and put herself to bed. Owen got the children into their pajamas and read them books.

"We're just the right size family, don't you think?" he asked them after lights-out.

"I want that hundred bucks in ones," Toby said. "Anyway a baby could sleep in here."

"I love babies," Paul said. "I love little, little tiny babies."

When later Sara moved her mouth down his body, and did her work there, he was only a little surprised. "I'm making good," she said. "Repaying an old debt."

She could not *make* him have another. She had the spigot, but not the—*I mean she had the faucet, but not*—he had his eyes closed, he was getting close. Usually—*always*—it went down the hatch. She wasn't shy about that, and he appreciated it.

But now her hand was there, near her mouth, and that was distracting, but then he gave himself over. He felt her—he did, he would think of it later with disbelief and fear—he felt her, well, *catch* it. Sort of. And while his heart slowed, she slipped off to the ladies.

In the morning, on the edge of the sink, he found the syringe with its smell of bleached leaves. There was still a trace of milky fluid inside, and he inspected it closely.

It was impossible.

Sara was humming. Sara was secretive and rosy. If she had done this thing, Owen thought, it would be the end. They were *adults* here. He tried to count backward from the day of her last cycle, or frontward from the day of her last menstruation, or whatever it was. By his reckoning they were safe, though that wasn't the point. That wasn't the point!

He would fight fire with fire.

A certain friend had recently recommended to Owen a certain doctor. It was a day trip to a clinic and a quick snip, the friend assured him, nothing more.

Owen waited a week, then made the appointment.

It was horrible—to keep such a secret from his wife. But she'd brought him to battle, and he kept the appointment, and it was hardly painful at all. And anyway—anyway, if you wanted to nitpick—well, the thing could be reversed.

In the meantime, Sara energetically whittled away at her debt. Again and again she filled him with joy, then caught and carried the gloop off into the bathroom in her bare slick hand, leaving the syringe on the edge of the sink each and every time.

As though they'd *agreed*. As though they were playing a game. The final time, she brought the syringe into the bedroom before-hand and placed it on the nightstand. And then, in front of God and everybody, she caught the stuff and used the syringe to suc-tion it from her palm. Then she stuck it up inside herself and smiled over at Owen, who was keeping his own secret.

At last the debt was paid in full.

It was impossible. He couldn't figure it out. There wasn't enough math in the world to make sense of it.

Because now, five months after his appointment, Sara was large with child. They might lose everything, for all she cared. They might need a larger house. And certainly, god-damnit—! they would need a minivan.

And did Sara care, did she?

Jesus, she was happy. She was so happy! Another baby was all she cared about! She just expected him to go right along with it. That was exactly the feeling he got! She expected Owen to lead her through the darkened towns on the back of a donkey, and knock on doors and face unfriendly occupants and scrounge up a spare stable and a manger and a burner to heat water on, for when the baby finally came, and a pile of rags in which to swaddle beautiful baby Lily.

She was beautiful, too, as it turned out, with a clear gaze and luscious lips. Paul, especially, was crazy about her.

In his mind's eye, in the stable, Toby and Paul skated around in the straw. Soon friends would appear, stepping into the circle of light to gaze down at the newborn. Owen wanted to shake his head in disgust. Didn't they realize that there was more to life than this, this urge to perpetuate their own wimpy set of genes? What were they all so hungry and desperate for?

And there was so much work in their future! Another five years, at least, of baby-proofing and toddler-chasing and childish demands! How could they endure it? They would go broke, they would break down, they would go crazy.

Sara offered her bare breast yet again to tiny Lily. The friends laid down their gifts and then drifted away, off to restaurants or romantic hideaways or sporting events where they sat rested and ringside.

"Stables don't have TVs," Owen imagined himself trying to explain to his sons. "In the olden days, people did other things. They played games at night. They read books. They talked amongst themselves."

The younger boy started to cry. The older one threw a fistful of straw into his little brother's face, and then they both started to shriek. *Me want tee-vee! Me want tee-vee!* squalled the younger son. The new baby wailed in alarm, and Sara cooed down at it and gave Owen a sleepy smile. The nerve!

The last friend congratulated them once more, then hurriedly deposited his gift with the others and rushed away. "See you at the gym," he told Owen, or something like it. The fact was, it would be years before Owen did anything normal. "Yeah, right," Owen said glumly as the stable door swung shut.

Then Owen was in his new life. It was warm in there, and smelled faintly of goat droppings. His wife and children were looking at him expectantly.

"Maybe we could scratch out a game of Hangman in the dirt," Owen said. He found them all sticks, and the boys thought up a word. Owen was hanging from the gallows with all but a single stickman leg before he finally guessed it. His sons were thrilled and terrified: *we almost killed daddy!* one said gleefully.

Then it was his turn. He thought up his own word, and soon there was a complete stickman dangling. But he kept at the game, adding fingers while his sons faltered, tearfully cast forth consonants. He drew ears. He added a moustache. He worked expressionlessly, giving the figure toes, then nostrils. They wouldn't hang; not any of them. There were tricks, for games such as these.

Some Women's
Hair

THERE ARE ALL KINDS of things that you find appealing. For one: her hair. It's spaghetti-squash yellow, pushed up hard on one side and falling to the other, making a wave. You've just read an Annie Dillard essay about waves. In these waves, enormous and illuminated with sunlight, Annie saw sharks. She saw the sharks in a feeding frenzy, trapped in the bright, hard, see-through crests; staring at her blonde, her hair, this is what you're reminded of. Tiny sharks. Appearing in her hair. Blue, caught, thrashing.

She wears a certain cologne; go find it. Go to the mall. You're helpless. You're in love. In the classroom she sweeps past and your heart sweeps along like a pinched-up hem, girlish and snapping, she's taken you with her. She has calfskin gloves. She has small eyes, so small they seem not to be able to take everything in, or at least not all at once. Anyway when she turns her eyes around the room, they glisten from the effort of taking it all in and the skin of her face is stretched back, pale, receding from the tiny eyes, to help. When she looks at you: in your lap your hands twitch with yearning. Try not to stare. Remember that she lives with a girl, lives like something on the bottom of the ocean, moving slowly forward, chuffing sand; a crustacean (no eyelids, which when you were a child was the most terrible thing: animals without these, cats and snakes for example) with hard red skin. That's how much you love her.

All kinds of little jokes occur to you. *Girl trouble. It's just that there's this* girl. *The most beautiful girl in the world, brings me candy.*

Once, just once after class, find an excuse to walk her to her car. She wears a long coat and the hem keeps flapping open, swatting your leg. Think of the possibilities. Think of her coat swaddled around your own anxious girl calves which are bare, speckled with cold because you would give anything to have her fall in love with you and so have worn this skirt to impress her, though it's for heaven's sake December.

Probably it's your only chance. You could stop walking and tell her exactly what you thought: maybe you'd say, you're the most beautiful woman I've ever laid eyes on, I mean it. Your throat goes tight, thinking this way. When she says something, smile blankly and shrug. Let her think you're an idiot, hairless, a moron.

She veers off toward her car, swinging one hand behind her back to wave. All the way to your own car, wonder if this is the way she says good-bye to everyone, her thin arms swinging like an athlete's and then one hand crossing behind for a peculiar, open and shut clasp of the hand. It looks so awkward on her body.

Smell your wrist. It's warm and has her smell, the one from the mall, and makes your eyes sting. Think again of the way she waved. Surely it meant something to her. Make another joke to yourself, say: *quit calling me Shirley.*

The Husband's
Dilemma

LET ME JUST TELL ya, his wife tells him, what a woman does not want at the end of a day like this one is to *be boned.* To be sunk the pink missile, to be *slipped the salami.* I'm not kidding. Can I just tell ya? She wants: (she goes on. *On and on!*) your average woman wants: *restaurant food.* Because your average woman is a jungle gym, a meeter of many tiny demands, one infant swinging from the nipple trying to get one last mouthful and the other two going *Candyland, Candyland, can't we play, mom? Please?* And she's been slaving, she points out, not to overdramatize suburban mania but she's been for example enriching the perimeter of some suburban plot with Miracle-Gro–infused topsoil and all that, steer manure, she's a stay-at-home, there's no Mexican guy being paid to show up and do it.

He has a job that's *big,* she reiterates, that's *important.* He also p.s. goes to lunch *every single motherloving day,* in a *restaurant,* where some woman *brings him his food.* Why does this stick in her craw?

Why do you resent me so much? He asks plaintively, sadly, such a good guy, truly, and she is after all a kept woman. No getting around that. Because did he want kids, did he? Was he the one? She wanted them, right? *So why do you resent me so much all the time?*

Restaurant food, she says again. It's the only thing that comes out. That ever comes out. It's the whole gist of the thing, that every day he has an *environment,* like maybe with Asian women moving past fish tanks, bearing trays.

So does the wife want him to *pack* his lunch? Is that what she's getting at? Like what, like a pee bee and jay? Like *tuna?* Is that what he's supposed to do? She is outlandish, truly, this wife of his. She bares her teeth; everything infuriates her.

Of course not, she says, of course you shouldn't take your own lunch, I'm not saying—. She backs off. I'm sorry, she says, I'm sorry, but I can't stop thinking about it. Restaurants with the tables that get wiped, the coffee topped off—there could be, though probably not at lunchtime, belly dancers. Were there belly dancers? she wants to know. A dish of butter mints next to the cash register? Or maybe someplace high-ceilinged and urban, with mounds of olives behind glass and sandwiches drenched in olive oil? She is so pissed off. The woman is so pissed off all the time! He thinks it must be, like, the signature emotion of motherhood. Jesus, why can't she get a life? Can she please just get a life? Please stop being ungrateful? His job is really actually hard! He manages employees! *Twelve!* Whereas her life, just in case anyone's asking, is wonderful but tiny, she reminds him all the time, oh can I tell you, it has shrinked to a rinkydink. No shit. If she could just take bong hits all day and let there just be shit all over the house, she says, *(on and on and on!* She reminds him of the woman in an antidrug spot on TV: the woman on her hands and knees, scrubbing, scrubbing, her eyes crazy, her pupils pinned, her hair wild: *I don't eat, and I don't sleep, but I've got the cleanest house on the street, Meth!* —, goes the voiceover. Which, when she saw it, actually made his wife say, *where do I get me some?)*, well then no problem. If she could just do Play-Doh and play tractor and watch Barney.

So why can't she just do that? Maybe he *should* buy her a bong. Glass, with a butterfly painted on the side. Because why does she have to sit around drinking so much coffee? Why does she have to want to be *brought things?* Why does she have to drink so much wine at night, starting from the minute he comes through the door? Why does she have to watch—I'm not kidding—*Little House on the Prairie?* What's up with that? Why does she have to take long, hot, searing— *searing*, like what if one of the kids accidentally fell in— baths? Why does she have to *shop?* Like that's some excuse? What's so important to buy? Birthday presents? Pots and pans? More mulch? Haven't they done enough mulching? Why does she have to go off?

She goes off: Shopko, Target. She's winded when she brings home her treasures, picture frames and panties and kid's shoes. These she is obsessed with: sandals, *swim clogs.* Is this what they've come to? Please tell me. A pair for each kid, six-ninety-nine a pair, a blue light special. *Thank god they had them in their sizes*, she says. Is she a sicko? Is she insane? When she gets like this, *he can no longer listen*: he's a husband wrapped in foam, a husband in a diver's suit and helmet, sunk in some aquarium, forever watching the lid of his tiny pirate chest bob open and closed.

I gave them chicken nuggets, he says.

And apple slices? Did they get apple slices? Already he's stepped in it, already he's left out a food group. He tries to kiss her and she veers off, frantic to file the shoe receipt in some little accordiony thing by the phone. She's obsessed. With minutae. She is minute. There is no way. No hope. No chance he can see of doing the horizontal rumba, later.

In the beginning, of course, there had been all kinds of screaming and swallowing. Like her trying to prove she was Good In Bed which translated to all sort of positions and athletics and moaning. The moaning! Like she was being slowly, pleasurably skewered. Plus she always wanted it: was that just a Girlfriend thing, as opposed to a Wife thing? Or maybe as opposed to a Mommy thing? He's not trying to generalize but here's the incredibly sad thing, how quickly his marriage has become a cliché. Sad but true. Plus: *plus*: she used to, if he may be indelicate, *swallow. She used to swallow.* Now, she pulls back at the last minute and sometimes gets it on the neck or sometimes gags, trying to swallow like in the old days but that's gone, that particular skill, she's washed up, a has-been. It makes her sad. It makes her cry. *I'm a hag*, she says. *A hag who can't even swallow anymore*, so that then he just feels worse and thereby have they pretty much avoided oral sex altogether. When did all this happen? Why did all this happen? When oh when did they start needing a tube of lubricant in the bedside drawer, for the babysitter to find when she snooped?

• • •

THE CHILDREN:

Oh the children, they are lovely. Two girls and a baby with round round eyes and cheeks and he is very brown, like a little Hawaiian. Each of the girls has a stick pony which when you squeeze on the ear makes a metallic galloping sound. Both ponies still wear their manufacturer's tags, which read: *thank you for purchasing the AMS stick horse with real sounds. Your stick horse leaves the factory with the switch in the "On" positions and will make realistic sounds when you squeeze the ear.* The girls, twins, are already tomboys, Powerpuff girls, future kick-ass babes. They are five. They ride horses all day. They have bangs. They make their Barbies go on campouts sans Ken. They make Barbie chop her own wood and build her own fire.

At night, he watches the porn channel on bootleg satellite. Well, porn *channels*. There are three: the Playboy Channel, Amateur Home Videos, and Luscious Ladies. Each Luscious Lady segment has two girls with shaved, dainty-looking slits and huge! huge! breasts that hold their pert shape even when the girls are lying back. Then there's some guy, it's like a miniseries or something, he wears clown makeup and has this huge! huge! dick that two girls take turns with. He wears this makeup and has on a clown wig and talks, for what reason the husband knows not, in a Wolfman Jack voice. Anyway, the husband selects a channel, then drags the curtains closed and pulls the shade down over the front door and gets to work. Except one time he forgot to turn the channel back, and the next morning, well, the wife comes out swinging. She calls him at work.

Guess what the girls saw on TV today? Kathy says, and now he knows what is meant by someone saying a voice sounded extremely *frosty*. We get up, his wife says, we all go in to turn on Barney, and instead there is some girl's *big butt right there on the screen*, and bobbing out of her *big slit* is a *dick*, do you think you could at least remember to switch the channels back so that instead of seeing Barney the girls see *that*, here we're expecting the Treehouse episode and everything, and do you think you could just at least please remember to do that *one little single tiny important thing?*

Sorry, he says, chastened. This is his *wife*. This is his precious beautiful *girl*. Who has turned sour. Who in the old days would make a joke of it at least. Like once when he said I watch the porn channel for poontang and she said, well, I at least hope you like your poon *tangy*. That was a pretty good one.

And Barney: who wouldn't want to try out a joke involving the porn channel and Barney? But no, now she just hangs up on him.

She is: *most unpleasant.*

Their yard looks good. He'll give her that. A-Plus for landscaping! His wife is no slacker. They have bulbs, they have flowering shrubs and a deeply rich green carpet-type lawn. *They have no weeds.* And the daughters, absolutely he will give her that, we're only talking about his being neglected here, the daughters play play play all day long and both can practically already read, plus they know how to swim. The house is clean and the wife does dinner, except sometimes when he picks up take-out Thai food, at which she is practically beside herself with pleasure. His theory is that she might be a big fat lesbian. Well, not a big fat one. But she is so *nice* to other people. She is so *nice* to *other women*. Which waitress helped you? she says. Was it that little one? Who always wears the pink sheath? She's so sweet, god I love her. Or was it the other one? The one who wears the Hair

Scrunchy? He has no idea. Some small woman. Some small woman with black hair and broken English.

Maybe she *is* a lesbian, his wife.

Of course not, she tells him when he finally works up enough nerve to ask. Yuck, *sex*, she says. I don't want it with *anybody*. Not even *myself*. It's so twitchy and spastic and unnatural. It's just so bodily fluid-y. I hate the thought. I wish I were Catholic, then at least I'd think it was my wifely duty. I'm sorry. I'm not trying to hurt your feelings. I just want you to know, it's not you. Maybe it's nursing, maybe it's just the kids, I'm just so tired tired tired all the time, all day long I swear I am, I know your job is hard, I know your job is hard, but I mean I just feel like I get shot out of a cannon every single morning. I can never just *relax*. I can never just *tune things out*.

That's true. He'll give her that. For someone who doesn't want sex she's like one giant nerve ending. She hears everything. She's taking in everything: the phone ringing, him telling her some story, the kids screaming, the TV.

Okay, so, obviously, with all this said, he's not making excuses for what happens next. It's his best friend's idea, Tijuana, just over the border to do some drinking; they're going to hit a pharmacy for whatever his friend can get his hands on, Neo-Percodan, whatever, the husband thinks, so maybe he'll just *ask* about something. Just *innocently inquire* about something that might put her at ease. He says *tranquilizer* to the pharmacist, but here's where the goof is, when he also lets out the word *wife*. He gets roofies, not Valium, though all this gets figured out later.

It could've been *worse*. He didn't do it on purpose.

He didn't say *Spanish Fly*.

But what he gets, he takes home and drops in her chilled glass of white wine (when he does it his hands are shaking; what if he kills her, I mean he's just *desperate*, that's how this all happened, it was just a bad idea all around, the husband lacking finally just like his five-year-old daughters so often do *impulse control.*). And it's not funny, no one's laughing, he could read, it said *Rohypnol*, he's no idiot, he knew what he was doing. But I mean we all make mistakes, right? A guy could do *worse*. A husband could cheat, or bring home genital herpes, or declare bankruptcy, yet none of that happened; he didn't even give her the full tablet. The girls were at a sleepover at Nana's and he just thought maybe, maybe he'd do it, the imp of the perverse had hold of him; he was *sick* of watching her maniacally weed yet again the flower bed, sick of watching her scour the kitchen counters in prophylactic yellow elbow-length gloves, sick of her not sitting down or propping her feet up or catching a movie, sick of her looking distracted and bitchy, sick of the *headset* she wears—did I mention, she wears a headset? *For keeping both hands free whilst making phone calls.* A headset, a cooking apron, and those yellow gloves—is she insane? She looks surreal. All of this drives him, drives him to do this one and final evil thing, to give his wife a roofie, or half a roofie, to bite it with his teeth and then watch it sink lazily to the bottom of her wine glass and bob like something injured when he poked it with the tip of the spoon, and then he stirred a while and carried it out to his wife weeding the flower bed. Make no mistake, he wants *her*.

Been watching the porn channel? she joked. Her hair was

loose, her jeans dirty from the garden but still she smelled like Victoria's Secret body lotion, his wife pear glacé–scented, not his first scent choice but okay, his wife ripe and sexy.

Baby, I've been watching the Kathy channel, he said then, he was desperate, did she just not love him anymore, was that it? But she shrugged even that one off. Though in the old days certainly she would've said something else, maybe *aww, you say all the right things,* and in the old days certainly one thing would've led to another, children or no children, there were ways, they could get a lock for the bedroom door, they could find a broom closet or rent a room at the Sheraton for one night or do it out in the hammock, they could be creative, it was part of a marriage.

Instead of him feeling all the time now like an employee. Like one of Martha Stewart's employees, actually. To put a finer point on it.

And so he gave her the glass, which she placed carefully on a flat rock before going right back to her precious weeding, said *thanks* but didn't look at him, and then he was *glad: he was glad:* and he went inside to wait, pacing in front of the curtain, checking on her; and then, worried, went out ten minutes later, where already she tilted woozily into him. He carried her across the threshold, hoping the neighbors, if they noticed, just thought they were being playful, the kids at Nana's so that maybe they were just renewing their wedding vows.

I feel sick, his wife said, and he felt her tremble against him. He carried her upstairs where abruptly she fought free to vomit, just making it to the toilet, well almost anyway, he could clean that little bit up later, was he a monster, what he wanted to do now, was he a monster? The way he unbuttoned so quickly, *you must be fucking joking* she said, *I want a glass of water, please will you get me a drink of water,* was he a sicko, he worked gently but worked all the same, getting her shoes off and she said *Honey, you desperate shit, if you want it so bad at least try it when I'm not puking.*

Kathy, is this okay? he asked, really needing to know, he wasn't a fucking *rapist* after all, he didn't want it *that way,* and she said *sure,* slurring, *if you're so horny just do it. Just pardon my puke.* And though there were things like repercussions in the world, things like decency and self-respect, he kept peeling away layers, her jeans, his shirt, her T-shirt, etc., he heard himself making realistic sounds, her eyes were closed now, and when he shook her a little she didn't stir. The water came up in his eyes then, and he stopped. She was his *wife,* she was his *wife.* He loved her, he should be taking her somewhere. Somewhere with a maitre d', somewhere with a *prix fixe* menu. Pear glacé–scented, passed out, still she is somehow so *menacing.* But not without a sense of humor, right? If it came to it, she would forgive him.

He's pretty sure about that. *She would understand.*

He pulls the curtains, strokes her arm, checks her pulse, which is steady. He weighs the pros and cons. It's a pity, the way she sleeps on, because right now, he thinks, right now, frankly? he could really use her advice.

Hannah's
Announcement

SOMETIMES IT SEEMS TO Ted as though he has spent his whole life driving, the road uncurling out in front of him like a party favor, his seat reclined. He's an hour outside of Spokane.

He flips the tape over and sings along, thinking about his wife. She had called him names: Asshole, Old Fogie, Son-of-a-Bitch. Not that he was innocent; Hannah's mouth, when it moved the way it did when she was calling him names, made him want to push it right down her throat. They had had their fights, with the girls hiding in the next room and Hannah taunting him, goading him, calling him those names and then throwing things: paintbrushes, coffee mugs, shoes. Ted had gone for her, swung at her; and he had been surprised, during these fights, at how abruptly and quickly his wife's body had shifted; how at the last minute she seemed to wriggle out of her ugly shape and into a new one so that when he'd swung, he would find knocked against the wall, his real wife; his sweetheart; the mother of his children. Afterward, he would wash her face. Bleeding, contrite, she moved under his hands exactly the way she had for eighteen years. He would wipe her nose with a washcloth.

I have got you under my skin, Ted sings, and taps his thigh to the music. He laughs partway through the song, unhappily, because it seems these days as though Hannah is just that: something burrowing into him, keeping him awake nights, skipping from his mind to his heart and then back again. She says *Ted,* in that bleating voice, says it right into his brain in the middle of the night and when he is on the toilet and when he is trying to read. *Ted,* as though there's something he's supposed to fix. Well, it isn't his fault. This was all her big idea, her plan, and even in the middle of his life falling apart he's supposed to drive to Spokane, sell textbooks, bring home the bacon and stuff it in the blistered mouth of his wife.

This is the kind of thing he hates himself for. That he didn't just say no, you bitch. Let Lars support you. But there are his girls.

Not that she would let him have any credit there. He takes these trips and when he comes back his daughters, his own girls, are afraid of him. It takes hours to coax them into safety, hours out of the one or two days he gets for visitation. Until the court decides, he's left feeling like some sorry beau, rushing home to Idaho Falls with all kinds of presents, standing in phone booths, trying to woo a little time with his own daughters. That's what makes him so sick. The way Hannah takes her time on the other end of the line, chomping on things, crackers and carrot sticks, saying she's trying to decide whether it's a good idea.

He visits his daughters in hotel rooms. The nicest ones he can afford, their favorite and his, the downtown Ramada Inn, with rooms that face out onto a courtyard. His girls sit in a line on the bed like children about to be punished, and this is where the presents come in. Last time, Ted brought them a pink shampoo that didn't need to be rinsed out. One by one, he had washed their hair and then wiped the pink froth from their heads with dry white hotel towels. *That's it,* Ted had said, combing Grace's wet hair, *that's all you have to do, now you just have to let it dry. Handy, isn't it? Isn't that something?* He had kept his voice light, indifferent, as though the shampoo were not what he knew it to be, magic, something he had seen in the drugstore (and then he had had to go to the bank, write out a check, return to the shop— that's how important it had been) and carried home to them, all these miles, a small bottle whose contents sloshed and frothed like his own helpless heart. How he had wanted to see their faces. And there was Grace, there were Caroline and Sarah and Mo like young seals, slick-headed and gay, making fun of each other's looks, calling things like *Hey, Slick,* and *Hey, Wethead.* And then they had cajoled him into it (though Ted had argued for a long time, saying he had no hair, the shampoo was for people with tresses; then he had pretended to have very long and lovely hair, tossing his head around and talking in a silly, girlish voice, saying *Rapunzel Rapunzel*) and finally he had wet his head under the tap and rubbed the pink stuff onto his own head, and wiped it off; so that he and his girls had gone down to the hotel coffee shop damp and giddy, like swimmers coming in from a lake.

Ted takes the next exit and drives two blocks to the orange rectangular sign: Denny's. He pulls into the parking lot and looks at himself in the mirror, running his fingers through his hair. He breaks wind, and thinks of his daughters shrieking and pinching their noses, saying *Dad!* He would hold out his index finger out and say *Pull.* And his girls would giggle with dread, inching forward to tug his finger, so that he could break wind.

• • •

"What kind of pie have you got, sweetheart?" The waitress is red-haired and efficient, with chapped hands from too much cleaning.

"Apple," the waitress says. "Cherry, blueberry, lemon meringue."

"Apple pie a la mode, s'il vous plait. What time have you got?"

"Eight-fifteen." The waitress takes his menu.

"Thanks," Ted says. "I don't want to get up tomorrow morning and find out I'm running an hour ahead."

"Do you take cream?" The waitress, MaryEllen, pushes her glasses up.

"Black," Ted says, and she moves off. There's a pinch in his back from all the driving, and Ted straightens, twists a little, sits back.

He supposes Lars is living with them. Though of course Hannah would never admit it, and he himself would never ask his daughters, put them in that position. Hannah has asked them to lie before, and he's seen the panic flit across their faces when he'd asked them things. He thinks of Lars with disgust, a fattish blond man in his thirties who would see fit to seduce a forty-year-old mother with four children. Lars has a beard, and talks through his nose; Ted can't see the appeal. The idea of that squat son-of-a-bitch sleeping in his own bed makes Ted feel sick.

Well, let Hannah have her cake. All he wants is his family. Hannah has taken to running around barefoot in long embroidered dresses (her hair also long, like a hippie's), and she laughs often when Ted comes around, showing her squarish yellowed teeth. She pushes her bangs back from her forehead and laughs right in his face, as though they haven't spent the last eighteen years of their life together. Not that he would want her back; not if she was offered to him on a silver platter. All he wants are his girls.

They've talked about their daughters as though they were property. Hannah would get Grace and Mo and Ted would get Caroline and Sarah. It seems fair. Still, it upsets him that Grace and Mo will have to live with Lars. If Ted could work it out, God knows he'd have every single one of them. Then Hannah could go off and do her thing, sow her wild oats while his girls grew up perfect as tulips, grew up and paraded their beauty before their mother's eyes. Ted can't imagine what she can be trying to teach them. He's seen *The Joy of Sex* in full view on the coffee table, though Sarah is just ten years old. What can she be thinking? The thought of the book being seen by his daughters is almost enough to make him turn the car around and drive back to Idaho Falls. He would pick up the book and wave it at Hannah, saying *What's this, just what exactly the hell is this?* She can't be that far gone. Even Hannah would know that this is something he could bring up in court, the same way he could mention to the judge that the mother of their children sees fit to have a different man in her bed every week. And that her breasts rattle around underneath the embroidered dresses like little animals on the loose. Ted pushes away the pie and waves at the waitress to bring him some more coffee.

"I'm brewing a fresh pot right now," MaryEllen says. She isn't bad-looking, and this time she smiles at Ted. He likes women with manners, women with modesty and clean mouths. When they were married, Hannah had cared about her appearance; she'd carried herself like a queen, and always shut the bathroom door after herself. But the last time Ted had gone to pick up his daughters for their weekend together, Hannah had yelled *come in,* and Ted had seen her from the end of the hallway, sitting on the toilet. "Excuse me if I don't get up," she'd said, and gave Ted the peace sign.

This, the sort of thing the woman who had been his wife for eighteen years found funny.

It was true that he'd asked her not to work. They had four girls to raise, and he was already gone so much of the time; who would take care of the kids? But it was more than that. Plainly, it just seemed wrong. He'd thought again and again about the house standing empty all day long, the turquoise tweed furniture in their living room empty, useless, like the furniture of dead people. That had been it, Ted thinks, swabbing a piece of pie crust through the melted ice cream, his house empty as a museum, leaving him nothing to think about coming home to. Not that he had been entirely selfish about the idea of her working. Because what would she do with the girls? Though he supposed she could've found a daytime job. These days, Hannah spends every night at the typewriter while the girls fix macaroni-and-cheese and fight over the TV channels. Hannah is typing her way through grad school, getting ready to become a high school principal or some damned thing. Typing and typing, like someone driven.

"I had pie a la mode," Ted tells the hostess. "And coffee. She never got around to bringing me my check." He pays for it, and rolls a toothpick from the dispenser. "Where's the closest hotel, sweetheart?"

"Coachman's Inn, down this way two blocks and then make a quick right." The hostess takes a cardboard box full of miniature peppermint patties from underneath the counter and fills the basket next to the cash register.

"Is it pretty nice, then?"

"We send a lot of people there." The hostess smiles at Ted. He feels embarrassed to have suggested that she would be familiar with the place. She looks like a nice married woman.

"Thanks, dear." Ted takes another toothpick and stashes it in his shirt pocket. Hannah could have been like any one of these women: courteous, and pleasant to watch, and not finding hidden meanings in everything. Hannah was always saying: "Oh, more innuendo?" in a sarcastic voice that made him want to drag her into the bathroom by the hair and wash her mouth out with soap.

He supposes Lars finds her remarks clever. Probably he chimes right in with his own, his nasally voice singsonging over the powder-green linoleum that Ted himself laid seven years ago, the highest quality they could afford at the time, Congoleum.

He could always steal his daughters. Ted settles onto one of the double beds with the ashtray on his chest, smoking, considering this. Of course he would never really do it but the idea tempts him, driving up to the playground one afternoon at three-oh-five, ten minutes before the school bus is scheduled to take them home, and his daughters could slip right into the backseat. And then he could take his family somewhere: Billings, or Sioux City. Of course he would never really do it, even Hannah knows that. She's screeched it at him a million times, telling him she'd have his ass thrown in jail, if she ever found him, if he ever tried to do such a thing, she'd make him pay for it 'til his dying day. Plus the fact that as much as he hates her, she's the mother of their children. Plus the fact that a deal's a deal; she'd get Grace and Mo and he'd take Caroline and Sarah.

Not having Sarah around has been one of the hardest things. She's always been his favorite, the one who'd tell him what Hannah was up to when they took car rides together. And Sarah was as sentimental as he, and together they would sing along to songs on the radio, and often stop for a piece of pie or a donut. He misses Sarah terribly, and thinks that he'd like to telephone. But when he does they both start to cry, and so it was better to just stay on the road and do his work until he could get home again. His most precious daughter. What wouldn't he give to have her here, clowning around and asking if they could watch Sonny and Cher? They'd always watched it at home, with Sarah strutting around and around the king-sized bed, pretending to have hair down to her waist, while Ted mimicked Sonny Bono singing in his reedy voice.

He's always felt guilty about playing favorites with Sarah. Ted had heard her flounce at her sisters during arguments, telling the others that her father loved her more; and then he would have to go in and tell her to her face that it wasn't true, that he loved his daughters equally, but in different ways. It wasn't right for Sarah to go thinking she was the only one he could love. Though Hannah herself plays favorites: she calls Gracie her Angel, Angel, sent from heaven to her poor mother, Gracie her only happiness.

He could telephone. Ted thinks of Lars picking up the phone in the kitchen of Ted's own house, quacking into the receiver. The son-of-a-bitch.

He takes the pillows from the other bed and piles them behind himself, then removes his belt, drapes it over the back of the chair, and unfastens the top button of his pants. He's gained some weight; still, he prides himself on other things, his posture, for instance, and the small attentions he continues to pay himself: the shoe shines, the weekly haircuts and teeth-cleaning. He's always been neat; and thinking this about himself, Ted goes into the bathroom and plugs in his electric razor, runs it carefully over his cheeks, his jaw, then applies his after-shave. He urinates, and thinks of Lars approaching Hannah like some rhinoceros, his penis thick and Scandinavian and menacing. Under him, Hannah would stretch and flatten the way she had all these years with Ted, making him feel like a million bucks, making him feel like a loved man, one who took care of them and locked all the doors and made her cry out and left him almost impossibly happy.

He flips through the TV channels for a minute, than dials Denise's number.

"Hello?"

"Hi, sweetheart." Ted lights a cigarette and settles onto the bed. "Am I taking you away from anything?"

"Ted!" Denise says. "You're here. Where are you?"

"Coachman's," Ted says. "I had dinner and came up."

"You should've come here," Denise says. "You don't need to do that. Stay in a motel. That's silly. Why didn't you come over here?"

"It's late," Ted says. He's wishing that he had driven straight over, in spite of knowing that it's a bad idea; at least, if Hannah ever found out, she'd have the book thrown at him and that would be that, no custody, no nothing. "It was late, is all," he says again.

"That's silly. Come over. We're watching Carol Burnett, you love Carol Burnett. And there's pumpkin pie. How are things?"

"In Idaho Falls, you mean?"

"Has anything been settled?"

"I don't know. I guess." His eyes fill abruptly with water, and his chest contracts in a single, bitter squeeze. He is lonely, lonely. "Maybe I'll come over."

"I'd like that," Denise says. "Bring your things."

"Is Al there?"

"He's here," Denise says. Al is Denise's teenaged son. "Is that going to influence your decision?"

"I just wonder about staying," Ted says.

"You can wait to get up until he leaves for school, in the morning," Denise says. "We'll be sneaky. It'll be fun."

Ted wishes that Denise sounded a little less eager. She's younger than he is, perkier, with unblemished skin and an enormous white smile. Denise teaches high school, and they had met when he'd come to Spokane three years ago. He'd shown her the history textbooks his company had to offer, and Denise had trusted his input, his opinions about which books were the best, and after Hannah had filed for divorce, he'd called Denise and asked her to dinner. She was not his wife; but then, he could never be her husband, a physics professor who'd published several books and who looked, from the photographs in Denise's den, exactly as Ted might have expected: heavy glasses, his hands girlish and long, a fellow so busy thinking about things that he couldn't even take the time to button his jacket properly. And then decapitated in a traffic accident on the interstate, when he was thirty-two.

"I'll get ice cream," he says. "Vanilla?"

In the night, Ted wakes. Denise sleeps near him, and he rests his fingers on her spine. He listens to the refrigerator come on, hum off. He's always been a heavy sleeper, at least until recently, and it annoys him tremendously to find himself now coming awake at the slightest sounds, like a man who can't find peace. That's it, he thinks. That's it exactly. They'd been good parents, every autumn buying jackets and boots for the girls, and then for themselves. They'd been a good family. And their sex life had been fine, even with Sarah sneaking to sleep between them, nights (so that finally they had had to put a lock on the door), even with their daughters all over the place, quarreling, skidding through the house in their stockinged feet.

Even in those days they had managed to make time for themselves. With the girls at school, Ted had showered with his wife, whose body had been round and soft as one carved from a bar of soap. He had lifted her up. He had spoken into the wet loops of her hair and held her, flat-footed, close.

He thinks again of having his girls, all four of them, living as much like a family as they could without a mother. Frankly, and he has been a long time admitting this, frankly, Hannah doesn't seem to like motherhood. Of course she loves their daughters, no question. But she doesn't seem to enjoy them, not like he does. On car trips his daughters were wondrous and loud, exclaiming at things: a rock formation, or a deer flashing off in the foliage, or even just the way the road curved. And Hannah, next to him, would sit very upright, clutching the dashboard, and when the girls leaned forward to grip the back of the seat she'd snap at them to sit back, stop pulling, they were pulling her hair. Then she'd gaze off out the window, like someone making plans.

Not that Hannah would be willing to give him a shot at being a full-time father; not in a million years. (*Over my dead body,* she'd say.) Because Hannah was all words. That was exactly it. No matter how much she might want her freedom, no matter how much she might want really and truly to be alone, Ted knows she'd never be able to get past the yammering in her own head; and as soon as the words started up, it was hopeless. Because Hannah, when it came right down to it, was as sentimental as he was. She'd start to think about letting Ted have custody, and Ted could hear it as clearly as if he were right there in her brain. *But they're my girls,* she'd say piteously. *My angels.* (This was the worst, when she got so involved that she'd hang that shit on their daughters—especially Grace—calling them her angels, her truth and salvation.) *They're my hope,* she'd said, not long ago. *I can't, I can't let them go.* She'd spoken the words to Ted across the kitchen table and he'd nearly wavered: had nearly said forget it, I won't even fight it, just take them all. You can have them all. But then he thought of Hannah, the way she laughed at their childish jokes like someone who was coughing and annoyed; and he thought about the way she'd tipped her head all those times in the car to see whether or not her hair was being pulled, even before she'd felt it. And he thought of his own life without them. That life was terribly quiet, and filled with empty evenings where his thoughts would turn to nooses and razor blades. He might be a lot of things: he might, as Hannah accused him, be a bigot and a male chauvinist pig. But he is a good father; a good father; he has been as interested as anyone could be in his children, and thinking this, Ted flops miserably onto his stomach, feeling the tears rush to his eyes.

That's the main thing, Ted thinks. To know, with all of your heart what you are and aren't good at, and then to live your life that way. Maybe he wasn't rich, and maybe he'd been a son-of-a-bitch as a husband, but nobody could take his goodness as a father away from him; no one could say that he had not laughed completely, with love and admiration, when Caroline and Grace and Sarah had presented their own episode of the Carol Burnett show; and Grace, playing Harvey Korman, had pretended to lose it during every single skit, smirking and snickering into the imaginary camera.

The next morning, from Denny's, Ted telephones. Sure enough that son-of-a-bitch Lars answers the phone, sounding like lord of the manor. The fuck.

"Hello," Hannah says. She sounds angry already.

"Morning, Hannah," Ted says. He thought that they had agreed to be amicable. He finds his toothpick and pushes it between the gap in his front teeth. "How are things?"

"Things are just fine here," Hannah says. She sounds nervous and brooding, like someone ready for a showdown. "Where are you?"

"Denny's," Ted says. He means to lighten the tone. "Eating strawberry waffles." He doesn't know why he's pandering to her. "I wanted to say hello to the girls. I have one library to do today and then a university to do tomorrow, and after that I'll be home."

"It's all over now, Charlie Brown," Hannah says. "I've filed for custody. I'm getting your ass on desertion."

"What?" Ted moves the toothpick onto his tongue. "Hannah?"

"It's all over now, Charlie Brown," his wife says again. "You don't stand a chance."

"Desertion," Ted says. "Hannah?" The toothpick, cinnamon, burns like a blade on his tongue. "You can't do that."

"I've done it, Ted," Hannah says. "You'll never see these kids again."

"What are you doing? Hannah? Why are you doing that?"

"You've been a bastard to me," Hannah says. Her voice shakes. "All these years. You bastard." She doesn't seem to believe herself; she says *Bastard, Bastard,* like someone rehearsing it.

"Let me talk to my daughters," Ted says. "Put them on the line."

"I don't want you upsetting them. They're upset enough now, as it is."

"I'll bet they are," Ted says. "I don't doubt that."

"Ted?" Lars says. "I think we all need to sit down and talk about some things."

"Get off the other end, Lard Ass," Ted says, and sets the toothpick on the metal ledge beneath the telephone. "I want to talk to my daughters."

"They're my children," Hannah says. "They need to be with their mother. So just stay away." Hannah snuffles into the phone, then she hangs up. After a minute, Ted hears another click: Lars's, from far away, in Ted's very own kitchen. Ted hangs up the phone and moves out to the car. He finds a packet of Rolaids between the seats and sits chewing the wafers, his throat tight, the sweet powder swimming on his tongue. He lets himself cry. He thinks of maiming his wife, really maiming her, though it appears, in his imagination, more like a cartoon: throttling Hannah until her eyes *sproing* out of her head, and then having them pop right back in. In truth, Hannah was a ferocious fighter; she had blackened Ted's eye, and once, swinging a saucepan, chipped his jawbone. The words sing and seesaw in his brain: custody, custody, desertion, desertion, and Ted starts the car, finding the freeway entrance.

He pushes a tape into the cassette player, trying not to let himself think. He is far from home, the miles straining against him like an incline, and Ted speeds up. He's gone only a few miles before he feels it, the first tightening of his heart, and he smacks his fist against the steering wheel, waiting for the pain to go by. He pulls over to the side of the highway. His heart feels like something retreating, squeezing and squeezing, and Ted clasps his hands tightly over his chest, as though his heart could shoot from between his fingers like a bar of soap. He breathes deeply, trying to concentrate on driving the pain out into his bloodstream, diluting it with his large body. The interior of the car is dingy as old snow. After a few minutes, he reclines his seat and gropes for the packet of Rolaids. Ted thinks of his daughters, lined up, waiting, their arms linked like the arms of small witches. They are playing Red Rover, Red Rover, and Ted runs across the lawn, ready to charge through their arms; but the arms of his daughters are stiff as quills, taking his weight. They are good at this. He can't break through.

The Birthday Party

IT STARTS THE WAY it always did: in and out. When you were five, when your sister was seven, there was this opening: between the beds, a big hole cut in the wall, a mouth to jump through, back and forth, when your mom might come to chase or spank you. Just some homeowner's way of being creative, I guess, this hole.

This mom wasn't much of a spanker. She rarely smacked you, and sometimes stopped halfway through to laugh if you could think up a good enough joke.

This mom had blessings, many: a swirled black glossy beehive hairdo, a nose sharp for cutting; teeth that looked like they could kill you but up close, up close, her soft mother lips slid softly closed. To protect, to whisper. Oh my lord, you should've seen the way she kept us. As tenderly as pastel rayon undies folded in a drawer. We would've done anything for her.

Little: there was this opening, see. A mother who poofed

our bums with baby powder except that we were young misses, not babies: by now we were eight! And these were never our bad parents. They were the ones who smiled and loved over each sister bed, like parents in a picture book. It was not the mom. It was not the most excellent and huge sweet dad. All you knew was the little sister who stuck green grapes up her own bum. All you know is the huge killer ghost man who comes to your sister in dreams when she's all grown up and this ghost has no mercy for whiny little children: he makes of her bumhole a storage place. For keys, for chapstick, for road maps. Guess what? She's a glove compartment, a junk drawer.

When your sister turns sixteen there's a surprise party, and she's the prize. You come on the scene accidentally; as it turns out, the line forms in your bedroom. The first one you see has brown hair and a moustache and is next in line for your sister. The second one's a blond, and bums a cigarette from the first guy. The third one has a marijuana-leaf belt buckle. When you walk in they all look at the floor, out of respect. They're standing in your bedroom! They're touching your Barbies, your horse statues! But so what? There are other things going on. On the other side of the wall, your sister grunts in her bed. She's underneath a guy. She's the party favor. When that guy finishes, Mr. Moustache waits a minute, then goes in: hear him climb on. Squeakity squeakity squeakity squeakity squeak.

Hey, the blond says. You got a lighter?

Light his cigarette with matches from the back of the toilet. Light it like in the movies and try to flirt, though you have no boobs. He ignores you, looks dejected about something. Play with your Barbie dolls. Have them prance across the floor and kiss each other; have them do flips and splits and be cheer-leaders. Shove one of them onto the yellow horse statue. This girl resists! Her knees will not bend, her legs will not open, she shoots off into space. Oh, boy. This is always ruining the game. To have to interrupt the campout or cross-country horseback ride to retrieve spoiled Barbies who smile up from the floor with tight legs, knees together, never sorry. Show her to the guy who's waiting; she's a tiptoed blonde with pointy titties and blue eyes: maybe she's his type. But the second boy comes out, and the third one goes in. Softly, your sister tells him hi. She's a place for loose change, for stale candy and cassette decks. Consider the way your sister's legs will split and pop, if spread. Spare her, spare her. Beg.

Static

I THINK THAT A dog must feel like this, sometimes—this complete—just by laying its head down and smelling in the fabric, a beloved.

I could happily never leave this room, though my lover appears to tell me that distortion is everything—hearing it from a song and then coming to the doorway to bring home the point—and surely true that our love is a distortion, a wrinkle in fabric that no amount of his inserting himself into me can smooth. The last time at a restaurant he wore a dress, and I had almost never seen anything so lovely. A dark dress, and his body a naked and muscled gift beneath, so that when I saw a photo of Donatello's David some months later I could not stop staring, they were so alike: his walk the way David's might be, all saucy schoolgirl charm. And later this same night at home he danced for me, hips making a small hula motion, hands in his hair, his face slit-eyed and crafty at this power. When he smoothed his fine torso I thought *corny*, then broke at how his hands moved like lovers over his belly, his rib cage. *We are sweet and rotting*, the hands seemed to say. *Grainy fruit plopped in yellow grass. Eat.*

How was it, in the days before he disrupted my heart? What did I look at, in the days before his face? Because I am watching him always now like a dog from my sprawl in the sunlight, going still when he strokes my hair flat or, more lovely still, plunges through the fur and back in time to my skull. When a friend tells me how she carries in her mind's eye a miniaturized picture of her girlfriend (*yes*, she says, *so that when I think her up she's standing in a certain way, with a certain expression, a smirk almost, and wearing a black hat*) I think that she's remarkably self-possessed. I don't tell her that he moves across my thoughts in pieces, random as these moments of rhythmic, drowsy stroking; and that I peer for him exactly as my dog, left outside, peers through the sliding glass door, her expression strained and foolish and lovesick.

I'm reminded of a line from a kung fu movie, appearing in tiny white letters across the bottom of the screen when a character asks *don't you scare of death?* And I think I do, I do, I think how my lover feels like a future and I scare of death plenty, the way my own mother scares and so has colored her hair for the last ten years a hateful shade of yellow, like doll hair, like trying to prove she's still holding all the cards. And he, knowing that we don't have time to fritter, spends much of his time spelunking, finding me out; when we're done, both of us have the kind of marks children leave on each other, Indian Burns and Titty Twists, and though we've entered each other in every possible place still there is never any way to get close, or fierce, enough. In bed each night I peruse his body for signs, pimples and scars and tiny brown scraps of earwax, as though these might explain something: yet daily we become less intelligible, our happiness a freakish happenstance, so utterly farfetched that I find myself waiting—for anything, anyone—to take him away and then turn to me and say plainly: *all gone.*

Instead I hoard things, brood senselessly over tender body parts. His head for instance, which could so easily be crushed; yet each day, brazen, it enters the world, chances crowds and car trips as though it were not a planet but an ordinary human bone cap. I want to make him wear a helmet. Maudlin, I know, to dwell, but if he'd been my infant I'd have known bottom-wiping and the soft pebbles of his testes and his first human sounds. Wanting to speak him before he himself could speak. Because how could I be so lucky? How could anyone? He has massaged my temples, holding my head in his lap. Above me his face is upside down and sometimes, massaging, he simply rests his mouth against mine while his fingers make slow circles near my ears. Sweetness, sweetness. A snail would find him by extending sweet slime knobs but I am less scientific, my hands love him too much to be cautious and so creep like perverts across the heat and sleep-smell of our bed, sink deep to the spongy fragrant skull, a forest, really, and if you were a flea you'd see: each hair a tree to step around. When I began to love him it came upon me like something dreadful or hideous; I wasn't glad at all, why should I be I thought then, knowing how soon his name would have the force of a bludgeon. A simple name of a few letters and a short sound, intricately stitched into my skin— I was undone by it. You could've hissed this word at me through the walls of a womb and I would've turned, stirred in

the saline to hear the sound that meant him. I knew that whatever happened, the particular clump of letters, his name,
would attach to other things. His name—Grant—both a noun
for him and a verb meaning, *to bestow.* It happens occasionally in the world that someone says *take for granted,* says *I'll
grant you that.* And how then I want to applaud at how my
day has just been beautified.

Is this how a dog hears itself spoken? By the sound of a
loved one's voice, nothing more. As a kid, the assignment of
naming pets overwhelmed me; I'd chew over the possibilities
for days until finally someone else in the family would inter-
vene, put me out of my misery long enough to say *we're just
going to call her Lulu, okay? Just Lulu.* But Lulu meant
things, and meant not calling the dog other things, Queenie
for example, or Angie; and if you called her Angie it meant
you could croon the Rolling Stones song into the dog's quiet
face: *An-jay,* you could sing. *You're beautiful. You can't say we
never tri-yied.* Even then it was the finding words for things
that messed things up. Better to be free-floating and witless,
like the child I read about in the newspaper who was not des-
tined to live in this world. The girl's name was Courtney Ann
but her mama instead called her *bitch!* all the time, between
the times she was hitting the girl, and when her daughter
blessedly died of a brain hemorrhage the neighbors told. Told
how Courtney, when the mama said *bitch!* would look up to
hear her name. I can picture the two-year-old baby blinking
foolishly in the direction of her mama's scorn. Afterward, the
mama took Courtney Ann's body to a graveyard, by then the
voices in the mama's head jabbering and yakkity and loud,
you can bet, and she left Courtney Ann's body on a hill. Left
it there and walked off, listening.

Or those twins, remember? It was the 1960s and they had their own language not even the mom or dad could understand. This went on until they turned seven, at which time they surrendered and got to appear on TV. After all those years, the dad theorized into the mike, they'd had a breakthrough. One of the black-eyed twins said hello. Hello and hello and hello. She said it in a tiny voice, looking ancient and unconvinced; viewers at home would just have to believe her heart was in it. After this, the twins waved helplessly. They were lovely. They looked like little Anne Franks. And then the other twin seemed to figure something out suddenly, she touched her tiny pillbox hat in wonderment and began to weep. Maybe she was beginning to figure out how even being able to say things in the world wasn't enough, how sounds were like stick-figure drawings for what a person might really mean. Maybe she'd figured out that now everyone could see her, and would expect things such as answers to questions. By the time the twins turned eleven, they'd forgotten every speck of their secret language. Like the mom said shrewdly, there was no more necessity. My lover and I went bowling once and I remember how from behind he was narrow-shouldered and intent, gauging his shot, and then the few steps forward and the pretty way one leg slid behind when he let go the ball. Then he turned and walked back to me, watching me all the way, and I felt like a million bucks. I was thinking a silly thing. I was thinking *Darling, I am a dog, I have loved you always.*

Mike
Incorporated

I KNOW AS WELL as anyone that you're not just supposed to choose your realtor from the Yellow Pages.

But I'm a little impulsive. My husband Matt and I decided to put our house on the market on a Thursday, and by Friday morning Mike was standing in the middle of our living room. I'd cleaned the place within an inch of its life. Every surface gleamed and smelled good and sparkled. Sure, I'd called a few friends to ask for recommendations for realtors. But their machines picked up every time and I'd already seen another house I was interested in. I know, I know. Anyone could tell you! When you go to make the biggest investment of your life, you are not supposed to be in some big fat hurry. It's just that I wanted this other place so bad. And I knew our house was nice, I knew it would sell. It was the *house* we were selling; that's how I saw it. How unsavory or bad could a realtor be?

So there Mike stood, jingling the change in his pockets and looking all around the house.

"Well," he said after a while. "I could do this. I could sell this place for you right quick."

So I signed the contract with Sealy Properties, Incorporated.

I was ready, I don't know—I was ready to *do* things. I spent Friday working in the yard, and Mike promised to bring a sign by and get the ad in the paper for Sunday. But the weekend came and went and I just kept getting *his* machine. And by then of course a couple of people had called back with realtor recommendations. But we'd signed, we were committed to Mike. And he showed up again unexpectedly on Monday, jangling change again, and this time whistling and saying he already had a prospective buyer.

"No way!" I said. The house that I wanted so bad was still on the market. It had a guest house and big old trees and a stream running through the property, and it was just barely in our price range.

"An old guy," Mike said. "Used to work selling vacuums. Made a fortune that way. He wants to come by later today, maybe say around three?"

That day I baked snickerdoodles. The old guy showed up, and glanced at the house before promptly dumping half-a-box of baking soda on my nice rug. Mike more or less ignored him, all the while sending winks my way. The old guy shuffled out to his van and came back with an ancient canister vacuum, still in its original box, and sucked up the baking soda and inquired would I like to buy a Sunrise canister vac with attachments and optional carpet cleaning liquid and canister, all on affordable payments of twenty-nine ninety-nine a month. This time when Mike caught my eye, he grimaced and shrugged.

"So what do you think of the house itself, Old-Timer?"

The guy said he'd have to think it over. He asked to use the potty. I showed him the way to the guest bathroom, and he followed along despondently.

"So will you at least think it over?" he asked when he came back. "It's been a while since I've had a sale, and you know. The old lady. She's beginning to doubt my abilities as a salesman."

"Pack it out, Old Man," Mike told him. "We've got real business to attend to here."

"I'll think it over. You bet," I said. I hadn't heard a flush when the old guy came out of the restroom. I had to go check. And flush for him, sure enough.

Meanwhile, Mike sat at my kitchen table writing up the ad. It sounded good, it sounded *great*. I didn't have the heart to ask him why he hadn't gotten it in the paper sooner.

"What say you and me swing down to the corporate office and pick up a sign?"

Corporate helped. *Corporate office* sounded perfect. A place with much activity and women rushing around answering phones and making copies.

"Maybe I could just stay here and get stuff done," I said. "Make the house look nice."

"'Give it curbside appeal,' you mean."

"Yeah. Exactly."

"Except, if there's no sign out front, how will people even know to slow their cars down? You look nice in that pink sweater, by the way. Not to make you anxious or hit on you. I'm a married man. But I'm one who believes in saying what's on his mind."

"Thank you. But look, I think I really will stay here. This

is really my only time to do housework. The kids get out of preschool at twelve-thirty."

"Well do you want to sell your house or what?"

That made me so anxious that I hurried to get my purse and my sweater.

"Thank you for the friendly and feminine cooperation." Mike said, and gave me a *thumbs* up.

I am not stupid. I did not appreciate that comment, not one bit.

And then began the selling of the house, or anyway the marketing of our small but entirely appealing bungalow. You can't tell me, even now, that it had anything to do with the house. The house lacked nothing. Matt and I had paid through the nose to have the kitchen redone a few years back, as well as the master bath. It was on a nice quiet street, with new carpeting and a large and fully fenced backyard.

That day, we picked up the sign and I stood off to the side holding it while Mike dug the hole.

"This is my least favorite part of the job," he said. "My wife Stephanie usually does this part but she had cramps today. *Cramps.* I am so glad I don't have some moon cycle. That's about all I can say."

"She must be pretty buff if she can dig holes like this all day long."

"Oh believe you me, she's cut," Mike told me. "She lifts. She could kick my ass. She's like the earth aspect of our marriage. I'm the fire."

"Could I just lean this against the house for a few? I think I heard the phone."

"I'm almost finished."

He wasn't, of course.

"I'll be back in a jif," I said.

Mike grimaced. "Suit yourself."

I called Matt the minute I was inside.

"I don't know if this is going to work out," I said. "This whole Mike thing."

"Really? What's up?"

"He just seems kind of needy. Plus he hasn't even gotten the ad in. I'm holding the sign while he digs the hole."

Matt laughed.

"It's not funny," I said. "I have stuff to do."

"Well just tell him."

"I *do*. I *have*."

"Well. We did sign the contract. "

"I know. I think he's lonely. I'm dying to meet his wife. She's a weight-lifter."

"I have a call coming in. Call me later though, okay? Good luck."

I watched Mike out the window for a minute. He kept resting on the shovel and retying the bandanna on his forehead. At one point, he wandered over to look up at the horse chestnut tree. When I went back out he was in the driveway stomping the skin off a few chestnuts and putting them in his pocket. "I used to love to collect these when I was a kid," he said. "Boy oh boy, thems were the days. Back when I had no worries."

"How's the digging going?"

Mike wagged a finger at me. "You *women*," he scolded playfully. "You want everything yesterday. Well, back at it I guess. You don't happen to have anything cold to drink, do you?"

Three days passed. Each day I drove past the house I coveted. Each day I did another thing to the bungalow to make it look nice. I rode herd with Matt and my three-year-old twins, Austin and Robbie, all of whom were extremely messy. If there were dirty dishes in the sink when Mike showed up with a buyer—two more, now, a slinking young couple and a forty-something divorced man with a beer gut—I threw them all right under the sink, and turned off the TV and slammed the entertainment armoire door shut and shooed the kids into the backyard and kicked shoes under the couch and raced around flipping on lights and tossing the unsorted mail in a drawer. I put on a nice feminine shade of pink lipstick and yanked both dogs by the collar into the garage, and heard the doorbell ring again while I scooped up the kids' latest science experiment—this time, sand and oregano and spaghetti sauce and raw eggs and blue food coloring, all mixed in a juice container—and stuck it in the fridge.

On the days in between, I improved the look of the house in every way possible. I put fresh flowers everywhere and tucked lamp cords under rugs or behind furniture. I vacuumed every day, and Windexed every possible glass surface. It was about impossible to live in a clean house all day long. It was like living in the furniture section of a department store.

"I wish you would not do this," Matt told me one night before bed. He was facedown on the bed with his arms behind the head of the mattress, trying to find the electrical outlet. "A man simply wants to read his magazine before bedtime. A man simply wants his lamp plugged in." He yanked out both citrus-scented Glade plug-ins and tossed them over his shoulder.

"It looks *horrible* with the cord stretched out across the wall. And please don't forget to plug those back in. I read somewhere that a prospective buyer's first impression of a house is its smell."

"So? Any more calls?"

"I'm not going anywhere else with him. He needs a girl-friend. He needs a dog. Every time I turn around, he wants me to *go* somewhere with him. Like go make fliers or go look at comps or go with him to his office yet again to pick up some piece of paper. He's supposed to be the realtor. He's going to make money on us. I'm sick of him already. The house on Woodward isn't going to stay for sale forever. It's too nice. I want him to sell this house and I want him to leave me alone."

"Your making it look this nice lately makes me not want to sell. Maybe we should just look into an addition."

"You can go straight to H-E-double-upside-down-hockey-sticks," I said. It was true, though. The past week, the house had looked and smelled so nice that it even made me want to reconsider. The books were lined up so nicely on the book-shelves, and every afternoon I baked cookies with dough from a tube. All the signs of real life, of everyday life, were just gone—the smell of dinner, the uncapped toothpaste, the messy magazines. Every day I spritzed the rooms with Lysol. Every night I turned on certain lights and drew the curtains just so before I crossed the street in my socks to appraise the house with a stranger's eye. And at *least* once a day, I counted the fliers in the canister that hung from the For Sale sign. If even one had been taken, I was jubilant.

The next day, Mike stopped by to look things over.

"Any calls?" I asked. There were two women in his car, talking and smoking, even though I'd always heard that realtors were supposed to keep their cars clean and fresh-smelling. "Is that your wife?"

"Both of them!" Mike said, and winked at me. "Yep. Steph's

in the front. I just stopped by to let you know we have a bite. Some couple wants to look next Wednesday, if that's okay."

"Next Wednesday?"

"Well, they're just sort of kicking the idea around. But the house sure looks terrific. Listen, I thought I'd run down to headquarters, pick up a few more fliers just in case. What do you have going on today?"

"Just the usual. But go ahead. I need to mow the back, anyway, before the kids get home."

"Do you want to pop over there with me?"

"I wish I could, Mike. Seriously. But once the kids get home, it's just mayhem."

"I could use your input on the flier. I haven't gotten quite as many calls as I thought we would by now."

"The flier looks really nice. Matt put pretty much everything in there, right? I can't think of anything else right off."

Mike strolled over to pull a flier from the canister. He studied it for a minute. My mind was going over and over all the crap that needed to get done in the next couple of hours: a call to the preschool, and dentist's appointments to line up, and how I needed to sort through the boys' clothes, get rid of the summer stuff and launder and put the rest in storage. The dogs needed walking, plus the lawn mowing and the fact that I wanted very much to make a salad for dinner. And go to the gym, if at all possible. The thing was, this was his job. I didn't want to go to corporate headquarters again. I'd been there three times already!

"Sorry," I said.

"Well then, let's at least go inside for a minute so I can jot down some notes. If you're really opposed to coming with and relaying it firsthand."

"Do you want to invite Steph and her friend in?"

"Nah, they're okay. They can gab all day. They practically got a cooler and a tent out there."

"Okay." I waved, and both women waved back.

Inside, Mike pulled up a chair and settled in. "Paper," he said. "Pen, please. Did you just brew a fresh pot of coffee?"

"I did." I'm marinating chicken. I hate having Mike in my kitchen. I can write a poem, but I can't sell my home.

"Stop, now just stop fussing for a minute. Come sit down. You remind me of my mother. She never stopped bustling around either, even when one of us needed to talk. She was always: cooking. She was always: cleaning. She would never just sit down!"

"How many kids in your family?"

"Five," Mike said. "I have no idea how they did it."

"There ya go," I said. "I would sit down, but I've got to do this chicken. So. The flier."

"You just need more help around here, is my theory."

"Any takers? But they'd have to work for cheap."

"I have ideas. I have a few. But we'll table that particular discussion for now, in order to get on with the sale of this here abode. Couldn't you just spare a minute to go over this? And then I'll be out of your hair. You look really nice in blue, by the way."

I sat down.

Mike read through the text of the flier and chuckled. "'Classy bargain,'" he read. "Was that your brilliant husband's idea?"

"We think it's classy."

"Okay, okay. I'll back off. But now, in your opinion what are the real strengths of this house? I mean I'm the realtor. I see what I see. But if you had to focus on just one thing, one detail or element that sets your house apart, what would it be?" Mike's beeper went off. He studied the number thought-fully, then took his cell phone from an actual holster he wore around his waist. It killed me. "Excuse me," he said.

I hopped back up. I was going to get tonight's salad made, even if it was over his dead body. *Well, just have Yolanda do it,* I heard him say. *Or ask one of the others. I'm at work here, you know.*

"I am so sorry," he said after he'd hung up. "Crazy home life. You know the drill. Did you say there was coffee?"

"Of course. Sure." I fetched him a cup. I was such an idiot, I hate myself. But Mike shows up, and I called him, and we signed the contract and now there is nothing for it but to tough it out.

"So the one unique thing about your house," he said, and sipped his coffee. "Do you have cream and sugar?"

"I don't know. Maybe the front porch."

Mike made a careful note of this. *Front porch,* he wrote, and underlined *front.*

"So, do you and Matt get along pretty well? Ya happily married?"

"We're crazy about each other," I said.

"Yeah. Me and Stephanie too. Look, it really would be easier if you could just come with me one more time. To the office. That way I don't have to take all these notes, then get there and sit down at the computer and try to decipher my own scribbling. That way we can add relevant information, get this baby locked in. What's with that place you're inter-ested in? Where is it, now?"

"Woodward. Just off Seventeenth."

"That's a superb area. I don't want to worry you, but houses on that end of town get snapped up." He looked down at his notes, underlined *porch.* "So nothing else comes to mind?"

"You're the realtor. You've probably sold tons of houses. We'll rely on your expertise with the ad."

Mike shrugged. "Have it your way," he said, and sighed. This was my day. This was my life. I'd lived through two C-sections, where I was chopped open and my bladder tore and I limped around for weeks after with a stinky catheter bag taped to the inside of my left leg so that even the dogs avoided me. I was the bitch in the house, the caller of all shots domestic, the queen of all that I could see. And still, because our future was in his hands, because I was too stupid to actually research realtors, I sat there acting like some idiotic little Kewpie doll.

"Really, we trust you," I told him.

"I don't feel entirely comfortable making these sorts of decisions without you," Mike said. "Maybe we could just quickly zip on over there together?"

"Oh shoot, I can't. I forgot, my sister-in-law's dropping her baby off this morning. She has to go in to work and I offered to help forever ago. You could revise the flier and then fax it. Maybe that would work, if you want feedback."

"When's your sister-in-law going to be here?"

"Around eleven."

"Great. We can be back in an hour. That'll work."

"Do you think you could just go? There's just a bunch of stuff I really have to get done this morning."

"Well, this is stuff I have to get done," Mike said. "It's so weird because, you know, it's your house. But okay. Whatever." He sighed. "So will you at least have time tomorrow?"

"You mean to go with you to the real estate office?"

"Yeah. So I get the information right."

"You want to wait and go tomorrow?"

"I don't want to wait, but I will. So, can you?"

"I guess."

"Great," Mike said, and scooped up his keys. "I'll pick you up at eleven."

I wasn't afraid of Mike, exactly.

And yet one way or another I kept winding up in the front seat of his Geo Metro, on our umpteenth trip to his office. FYI, the front seat of Mike's car was mighty interesting. It included, but wasn't limited to, a fat roll of cash wrapped with a rubber band, which he kept in the glove compartment along with three pocket knives. Why a realtor would have such things, I could not tell you. Also, several Mariah Carey CDs.

But I mean hello, hello in there Mike, can you see that we have a life here? We had two kids, two dogs, and four guinea pigs. It was true that I didn't have to actually go in to work every day, but I wanted every time Mike showed up for him to see, just *notice*, what your average homemaker did over the course of a day. It all looked invisible, I knew that. I'd been the teenager slumped uselessly on the couch while my own parents, especially my mother, kept things together around me. I'd been the friend in college who never understood why my married-with-children girlfriends could never just seem to sit the hell down. And now I was among them, one of them, a busy female in the background, a woman soundlessly and constantly in motion, and it infuriated me each and every time Mike showed up. The house had been on the market three weeks, and still there had been no offers, and now I was scheduled—*scheduled*—to accompany Mike to his office the following day.

My point was, I had a life here. I had stuff going on! After Mike left, I roamed miserably through the house, and looked over our contract again before finally retreating to mow the back lawn. I mowed it furiously, pulverizing several Happy Meal toys in the process. And then, because I was still so wound up and pissed off, I called Matt.

"'Classy bargain' is not working!" I shrieked at Matt as soon as he picked up.

"What?"

"He left. Mike left in a huff because I wouldn't go down to his stupid office with him again. He doesn't even have anyone lined up for the whole rest of this week to look at the house, and I'm supposed to keep it looking like this for god knows how long even when you and the boys are being pigs."

"Don't take it out on me that your fingers did the walking and you hired some incompetent. And I never said I was a writer. Shouldn't he have written the ad? I thought the realtor was supposed to do that."

"And now he's going to want ideas tomorrow. He's going to drag me down there tomorrow, even though I have about a jillion things to do, and he's going to make me sit there and look at the fish tank and spend hours trying to fix our stupid flier. Even though he even had his wife and some friend with him today, so that he wouldn't have to be alone by his precious self, which is what it's beginning to seem like. So you'd better start thinking. We need to come up with ideas. Because I'm not going with him."

"Maybe he has a crush on you. Maybe you're his type."

"Whatever. I swear I'm not going to go with him. I swear I won't. I'm going to tell him I have cramps or something."

"Well. We do just need to get it sold. We can't live like this forever. It's making you nuts. And me, by extension."

"It's like you want me to drive around all day with some insane realtor! Do you know that he keeps knives in his glove compartment? Do you know that he keeps a huge roll of cash with a rubber band? A *realtor.*"

"No way!" Matt says. "That's cool."

"It is not cool! I'm the mother of your children!"

"All right, okay," Matt conceded. "I'll ask around at work, see if anyone knows any other realtors. Maybe we can get out of our contract."

On his best days, Mike bounced in with boyish, frat-boy energy and clean hair. He was actually a decent-looking guy. The following morning he looked hopeful, and said he'd gotten no less than three different calls about our house. One couple, he told me, had driven by every day since the ad had appeared in the paper.

"So why don't they make an appointment to come look?" I asked.

"Bad credit," Mike said. "Which isn't the end of the world. People think if they miss one mortgage payment, their whole life is in ruins. But there are things we can do. We can write letters."

I'd planned to play the cramps card, but instead I just go get my purse. I even put on lipstick. I wanted to hear about the calls.

"Are you going to be too hot?" Mike asked. I'm wearing jeans and my Old Navy sweatshirt.

"I'm fine," I said.

"You might just be better off in shorts. My car doesn't have AC, remember."

"I'm great. Where's Stephanie?"

"Oh, it was her turn to watch the kids." Mike opened the passenger door for me. I'll tell you one thing I'd noticed: with Mike driving around, and with me in the passenger's seat, we looked to the whole rest of the world like a couple. I smiled and listened attentively and did things for him, wifely things, like telling him where to turn.

"You guys take turns?"

"No, I mean, she trades off with other wives."

"That's great. You mean like with the other mothers in your neighborhood?"

"Sort of."

"Wow. That's a great idea. Where do I sign up? That's totally cool."

"You think that's cool?"

"Trading babysitting? You bet. Takes a village, right?"

Mike was nodding vigorously. "That's right. That's so totally right."

"What is it you and Stephanie have? Four? Two sons and two daughters, right?"

"Yep. Are you and Matt going to have any more?"

"I want more, he doesn't. But we're probably done."

"Kids are great," Mike said.

"They are great. But so much *work*. That's why I couldn't go with you yesterday. Sometimes it's afternoon before I even get to do my hair. It's weird, because they're so wonderful, but we're both just sapped. I swear, every *wife* needs a wife. Or at least her own secretary."

"How's that?"

"No, no, I don't mean I think I deserve all this extra help. I have a great life. I just mean, it gets overwhelming."

"Amen to that," Mike said. "I wish more people thought like you. Look, do you mind if I go to the drive-thru?"

"No." I pushed the button to roll up the window, and then Mike took over with the button on his side. He rolled it up, then down, then up again, and smiled over at me.

"Want anything?" Mike asked.

"I'm good. I just kind of need to get home soon."

"Well I have to *eat*," Mike said.

"Sure, it's fine."

"Just get a shake or something. You're too skinny. What do I want, anyway? A Whopper or a grilled chicken sandwich? Which do you think sounds better?"

"So who were the other people who called?"

"Nice folks. Some skier from Germany who was looking for a winter home, and then some people with a mess of kids. I was thinking we could go back to the house and polish up the ad this afternoon, really get it looking perfect, before I called them back to come have a look. In the meantime you could do your thing, change into nicer clothes and get the beds made if they haven't been already, whatever, maybe hose off the driveway or whatever you think would make it look nice."

"I'm actually not going to be around this afternoon."

"Where are you going?"

"I just have some stuff to do."

"Stuff, huh?" Mike chuckled. He probably thought I was planning to spend the day at the mall. Chuckle on, Mike. I couldn't care less what he thought.

Mike pulled up to the window, and spent a few minutes flirting with the girl who handed him his bag. She was a spunky, high-school-aged beauty with very white teeth. Mike gave a low whistle as we drove off. "She was *hot*," he said.

"I kind of think she might be too young for you."

"Hey: no matter how old the bird dog, he still trembles when he sees the quail. Could you unwrap my burger and give me a bite? I'm driving, here. So, how long have you and Matt been married?"

"Eleven years? Twelve."

"You guys seem to like each other. Bite, please."

"Sure we do. We have a good life. How's Stephanie?" I held the burger so he could bite it, which I very much disliked doing. Holding it for him.

"She's pretty good. Do you know she can type a hundred words a minute? *And* take shorthand. She's an amazing specimen."

"Yeah, I'll have to meet her sometime."

"She wanted to meet you yesterday. She said you looked like you'd fit right into our family. Like one of us. She said you waved at her." Mike kept both hands on the wheel and leaned again my direction with his mouth open. "Bite," he said.

"He's a freak!" That was me in my next phone call to Matt.

"Did you get the new fliers all made up? How was that trip to the office?"

"Great, except that he wanted me to change into shorts. Great, except that then I made some crack about needing a wife and he looked at me totally weird and probably thinks I'm some lazy kept woman who can't even keep up with running her own household. And you know why I can't? Do you know why that is? Because I'm too busy running errands with *him*. Plus his wife thinks, as he puts it, that I look like one of them."

"What's that supposed to mean?"

"I think they *swing*."

"No way!"

"Way."

"Cool."

"It is not cool!"

"Got a call coming in," Matt said.

Later in the week, I got a call from Mike about some people who wanted to come see the house over the weekend. Two different parties, actually. "The ones that will be there at ten A.M. are the ladies," he said. "Maybe they're a couple, I didn't ask. Yolanda and something. I forget the other one's name. Anyhoo. And then the next people were just ones who cold-called. They said the afternoon would be fine."

This put me in a fine mood, especially since I'd been irrationally mad at Matt, who'd gone to Miami on a business trip. I had no idea what Miami was like but one thing I knew was, he'd be able to order room service if he wanted to, and take a dip in the sauna and schlep down to the bar for a nice, dry martini if he felt like it. But he supported us. He was basically paying me to live this nice life. So I tried so hard and all the time not to think this way.

"Mike, thank you thank you thank you!" I said. "We'll clear out. I can take the kids to the park or something. Or take them to their grandparents."

"I'd prefer you were there," Mike said. "If it's all the same to you."

"Don't you think they'd rather I wasn't hovering?"

"Well," Mike said. "The thing is, I'm kind of going to be out of town for the weekend. I thought you could show the house better than I could, so."

"You mean you're not going to be here?"

"That's what it's sounding like!"

"But you're the realtor."

"And don't you forget it, sister. Still, I've been planning this fishing trip for a while. You wouldn't have to do much, just show them around and maybe give them some history of the place, let them know whether you'll come down on the price or not. If they ask about whether you're leaving certain appliances and whatnot, you can decide all that with Matt beforehand. Just don't sign anything, know what I'm saying? If you don't sign anything, they got nothin'."

"What if they want to make us an offer?"

"Nothing happens on a weekend, even in real estate. You give them my number and ask them to call me on Monday and we go from there."

"Mike, I'd really like you to be here. You know we want that other house. You know we *really* want it."

"Can't buy that one until you sell yours, though. Right?"

"All right, okay. I'll show the house."

"The first people at ten, the second group around noon," Mike said. "Bank on it. Now, do you have any time this afternoon?"

"What *for*?"

"Don't sound so delighted. We could make it quick. I just need to get you a few documents, the appraiser's report and comps. I could swing by, take you over there and run you home."

I knew better than to ask that he just bring the papers himself. "By noon. I have to be *back home* no later than noon, okay?"

"Don't get your drawers all in a tangle," Mike said. "I'll see you in ten."

We hung up, and I went straight to the file drawer to review our contract. Sure enough, we'd promised to give Mike three months minimum to find a buyer. There was my signature. There was his. I went to the medicine cabinet and took a Xanax, then sat on the couch with my purse, waiting for Mike.

"Tell me a story or something," I asked Mike on the way to his office. "I think I've about got our route memorized."

"So one time, when we were all in a cabin in the mountains, I heard a noise late at night out on the deck," Mike said. "And I looked outside, and here was this big black dog rummaging in the garbage cans. And I think, whose dog? Since there weren't any neighbors for miles. But the kids always wanted a dog, so I go and get some sliced ham and some cheddar cheese and bread and I step outside."

"You were planning on making it a sandwich?" I said. "What kind of a dog?"

"I don't know," Mike said. "I thought maybe part Lab."

"Did he come to you?"

"So I step out there," Mike said. "I'm holding out this ham and whistling. And it looked up at me, only it's not a dog."

"Well?"

"It was a *bear!* Jesus, you should've seen me backing up. You should've heard that door slam."

"You should be a writer," I said. "You're a wonderful storyteller. Anyone else would've said, 'So there was the bear out on the deck, but I thought it was a *dog*.' You told it just right to keep the tension."

"Thanks," Mike said. "But Betsy's the writer in the family."

"Is Betsy your daughter?"

"No, no," Mike said. "She's actually a good friend of Stephanie's. But she feels like family. You know."

"What made you want to go into real estate, anyway?"

"Oh, I don't know. I always liked meeting new people. And

I've always liked, you know, seeing how everybody lives. The pictures around their house and the tables they eat at, all that. That sounds weird, doesn't it? Not like I'm some stalker. But I do. I like to see it."

I waited in the car while Mike jogged inside. Then he drove me home. "Hey, thanks for the company," he said when he pulled into the driveway. "I mean it. I'm a good realtor, but I know sometimes I can get up in people's faces, you know, in their space. I try not to. But anyways, good luck on Saturday. You'll sell the place. It's a sweet little home-sweet-home."

I was so set for Saturday. *So* set. I did absolutely every single thing I could think of to make the house look good. I dropped Austin and Robbie off at the grandparents', then came home to wait. Just before ten, I made a pot of coffee and popped some cinnamon rolls in the oven.

The doorbell rang at ten on the button. One woman introduced herself as Yolanda, and the other was Betsy. I showed them around, yakking up a storm. I guessed they were a couple, and I was looking for a chance to put them at ease. But I couldn't think how to do it without asking them straight out how long they'd been together, and I'd made that mistake before. So I kept my mouth shut and showed them every single feature I could think of.

They loved the yard. Yolanda took up residence in the hammock. "So, where you guys moving to?" she asked, and kicked off her sandals.

"Well. That depends I guess on whether we get an offer. I'm crazy about this other place, but. We have to wait until this one sells."

"Are you prequalified?" Betsy was on the patio, checking

out the hummingbird feeder. I couldn't think what else I was supposed to show them or tell them.

"What do you mean?"

"Prequalified means you're financially ready to get right into the next house," Yolanda said.

"Crap, I don't know. I'll have to ask my realtor."

"Yeah, ask him," Betsy said. "That's kind of like a huge deal. He should've remembered to tell you. Anyway, what makes you even want to move? This place is gorgeous."

"Oh, I don't know," I said. "I read somewhere that moving from one house to another was a married couple's way of getting a thrill. Of injecting new life into their relationship. I don't know. We do want a bigger place."

"Whoa, trippy theory," Yolanda said. "Are you guys going to have more kids?"

"No." I wanted to ask whether they had kids, but I thought it might open a can of worms. Maybe they weren't a couple. "Well, if you decide you like it, make us an offer. I need to call my realtor to ask him about the prequalifying."

"We'll get out of your hair." Yolanda stood up and stretched. "Yeah, ask him," she said. "That's important. You have to keep those real estate agents on the ball."

After Yolanda and Betsy left, I tried again and again to call Mike. No answer, of course. He was somewhere in the woods. I had an hour before the next people were going to show up, so I swung by my dream house on Woodward. "We're actually thinking of making an offer," I told the agent.

"Are you prequalified?" she wanted to know. "You don't stand a chance otherwise."

Which was how I wound up at Mike's house, on his front

porch, ringing the bell like crazy. I thought I'd at least tell his wife what I thought of his real estate skills. But it was Yolanda who came to the door.

"Uh-oh," she said when she saw me.

"Yolanda!" I said.

"I'm actually Stephanie," Yolanda said. "Sorry."

I tried to piece it together. Maybe Yolanda/Stephanie was Mike's wife, but then she'd fallen in love with the other woman, Betsy, and now they needed somewhere else to live. Then Betsy appeared in the hallway behind her and Betsy's mouth dropped open. "Busted," Stephanie told her.

"What the hell!" I said.

"Don't get mad. I can explain," Stephanie said. "I know it doesn't look good. But we really weren't just jerking you around. We were considering you, is the thing. I swear there really are serious buyers coming to look at your house later today. I *promise.*"

"Considering me for what?"

"Well, to be one of us," Stephanie said. "Come in for a minute so I can explain. You're not going to hit me or anything, right? Fucking Mike, he *would* go fishing. That's so typical. And leave the dirty work to us."

"Whatever your deal is, I don't want any part of it," I said. "I have no idea where Mike is. I have no idea whether you really wanted to buy our house or what. But if you see Mike, tell him he's fired."

"Oh come on. Chill."

"Well are you really interested in the house, or what?"

"Kind of not really."

"Well then what is your *deal?*"

"Our *deal,*" Stephanie said. "You make it sound so unsavory."

"If I wanted a threesome, I would've had it by now," I told her. I could see Betsy in the hallway behind Yolanda, listening. "I'm married. I like my husband a lot. We want to sell our house, this weekend if possible. And I have no idea what Mike is thinking or you guys are thinking or what, or if he just goes around posing as a realtor and you follow after him looking for chicks for him or what. And I'm sorry to have to say all this to you but now the house we really wanted is practically sold to someone else and I just think you're a bunch of perverts." I started to cry, and caught myself looking at my watch. Some part of my brain was still worried about when the next people were going to look at the house. But for all I knew, they didn't even exist.

"*Perverts,*" Betsy said. "What do you take us for? You think we've been cruising on you for a *threesome?* You can kiss my butt!"

"Well what else am I supposed to think! Are you a bunch of Wicca witches or what the hell? Are you selling Amway? Does Mike even have a real estate license?"

"Ow," Betsy went. "Ow! *Amway.*"

"'Kay, I think we've been insulted enough," Yolanda said. "We were considering you, true. For a sister-wife. But now you're officially uninvited." She shut the door in my face.

"Polygamists!" I told Matt. He was in a meeting, but I beeped him out to tell him.

"What? Who?"

"Mike and Stephanie and Yolanda. And Betsy. I'm pretty sure that's all of them."

"No way! Oh my god, that is the greatest thing I've ever heard. That's perfect. That is *fantastic.*"

"No Matt, it is not perfect. It is not fantastic. I called them a threesome. I called them witches. That other place I think is already sold, or on its way. I can't believe it."

"What made you think they were *witches?*"

"None of this is easy for me!" I yelled. "Come home, why don't you!"

"What a *story.*"

"They don't even look like polygamists. Not even remotely. The women are babes. I don't get it. And they have all this energy. All of them."

"I need to go here."

"I know, sorry."

"'Our realtor was a polygamist.' Only in Utah."

"You're just lucky," Stephanie told me when I appeared on the porch a few hours later. "Lucky we're so forgiving. Lucky we really did genuinely like you. Did those other folks ever show up?"

"Take a wild guess," I said.

"Well, no worries. Sealy Incorporated is on the ball."

There were cars pulling up at the curb, several, and men and women with nicely styled hair and clipboards hopping out. "Don't freak out, this is what's called a real estate Caravan. Of course Mike's a real realtor. We called the office and the other agents agreed to come look at your property today, see if they can get a few interested parties in here. I promise it's official." The other agents were coming up the walk, smiling and offering me their business cards. "Mike's odd, but basically a good guy," one of them, Laurie Rieser, told me. "He'll get your place sold." They swept past me talking about MLS listings, whatever those were.

"So look," Stephanie said. "We kind of thought you

understood what was going on from the beginning. Mike told us he told you you'd fit right in with our family, and how you seemed to kind of agree, and we're usually not this forward, not like we go trolling for other sister wives or anything, but he just really took a shine to you."

"Nice," I said. "Really nice for me."

"So big whoop, we're polygamists. Gotta love what people assume about us. Like we're a bunch of hot-tubbers instead of just people who've figured out that polygamy might actually be a good thing, a progressive thing that actually serves everyone involved. That it's a feminist thing. But whatever, you don't care, obviously you're not interested, obviously you think your insular little nuclear-family-unit thing is so great, even if there is a whole lot to be said for our lifestyle, considering how every time I see you, you look about *frantic* with stuff that has to get done. Whereas, like in our case, when there's more than one wife working, well: you do the math."

"All right, listen, I'm so sorry. Can we please at least just get this back to a professional level? I blew it. I'm sorry. I don't care what your lifestyle is, I swear I don't. We just want to sell this place. I'm flattered you're considering me." I was eager to be with normal people, realtors who actually might have legitimate questions about, say, the warranty on our furnace. They were all over the house, making enthusiastic exclamations and taking notes.

"Were considering," Betsy said. "*Were.* Past tense."

I saw Mike the next day for the last time. They all showed up: Mike, Stephanie, Yolanda, Betsy, and about six kids.

"Thanks for making cuts about my whole life," Mike said.

He made a production of tearing our contract into little pieces, which he left all over the front lawn.

"Sorry about yesterday," Stephanie said. "I can't believe you didn't know!"

"*I'm* sorry about yesterday. Anyway, how would I know? You're the first polygamists I've ever met."

"We're probably actually not," Yolanda said. She'd brought along some yellowy dessert. "Here's a peace offering. We felt bad about lying and wasting your time yesterday morning. But some of the other agents really will be calling. Maybe one of them can represent you guys."

"It's not like we all, like, sleep in the same big bed," Stephanie told me. "We share him. We take turns."

"And now, how many kids do you have? Where are they?"

"With Tina."

"Who?"

"You haven't met her," Stephanie said.

"Don't you guys get jealous?"

"Hell no!" Yolanda said and laughed. "What we want to know is, how do you keep from getting a yeast infection?"

"It doesn't *hurt* when you do it right, thank you very much," I said.

"You just keep telling yourself that, honey," Betsy said. "Really, you should be totally flattered that we considered you. That doesn't happen very often. But you were giving off some sort of a vibe."

"What kind of a vibe?"

"Like an I'm-resentful-because-my-husband's-never-home - and-I-wish-he-were vibe," Betsy said. "A no-one-even-notices-the-puny-crap-that-I-do-that-basically-isn't-all-that-important -or-interesting-and-so-basically-goes-unnoticed one. We can relate. That's why it works so well for us. Thank you, by the way, Stephanie, for thinking to bring her dessert. That was a very thoughtful gesture."

"You're very welcome, Betsy." Stephanie turned to me and smiled. "See how it works?"

"I kind of don't."

"Your loss," Betsy said. She carefully picked lint from her sweater. "You'll never know."

I tried to imagine their life, the one in which this or that wife moved down the hallway on her given day, slipping noiselessly past the children's rooms. She carried a candle and wore a thin gown. She was fresh from a deep hot bath, where she'd taken the time to exfoliate and moisturize. She opened Mike's door. He was so energetic, so needy! In other rooms, the sister wives read books or had already drifted off to sleep. The pets were all fed, and the lawn mowed and edged.

In my head, Mike went *Which do I want? Which do you think sounds better?* And for the life of me, I couldn't think how to answer.

Immolation

YOU COULD EXPERIENCE HER as the Angel of Death. And all she was was a skinny girl with flyaway black hair, working a cash register like it meant something. So what would there be to love? She was foulmouthed, she leaned against the counter and took everything in from the corners of her eyes. She wore ugly blue shimmered tights, and blue shimmery eye shadow to match. She called you "Boy."

And reminded you of every Stuckey's you'd ever been in, driven away from. When you were a boy, Stuckey's was where your family stopped to buy divinity candy on long car trips. Your dad pumped gas, smoking a cigarette with his eyes squinched, being careful not to splash his shoes or the front of his shirt, which would send him up in flames. In the backseat of the Buick, you sat coloring. Your mom bought the divinity candy and paid for the gas and came out with the box of candy tucked up into her armpit, her hair blowing, being careful with two small white cups of coffee. She loved you all.

The cashier brought on memories, wrathful. She would never love you. When it came time to step up and buy your own white Styrofoam cup of coffee, the girl exhaled smoke and called you Boy and then went on her break just like that. No warning. The girl, Jo, made the next clerk wait on you. Just like the time your mom went to the bathroom and you waited and waited. You sat in the car while your dad smoked. Maybe she'd had to borrow a key on a huge metal hoop, you'd reasoned. Maybe she'd had to go number two. Two kids coloring, one dad smoking and looking from time to time over at the cinder-block building with signs for Ladies and Gents. You had a dad with great patience. He smoked three cigarettes before finally going inside.

When he's out of earshot, hit your younger brother; steal his Burnt Sienna Crayola and draw poop-colored slashes over the frog he's just painstakingly made plaid. Your baby brother, stunned, breaks into puny, slurpy sobs. To apologize, to make him love you all over again, give the snail on the opposite page a most beautiful pair of pale green wings. Swoop the coloring book back and forth over your poor dumb brother's head. This is making the snail fly. If it could, the snail would be oozing goo, having dragged its sorry slow body off the edge of the sidewalk and crashed into the grass at the edge of the lawn. It was summer, you were ten, and this small drama happened almost daily: the pause, the sticky, sensuous roll back to life. Sometimes, lording over a stretch of sidewalk, you'd let such a snail pass, but more often you blocked its progress, making a dam with your hand so that it waved its antennae curiously and sadly up at you.

That year for Christmas your mom will send Sea-Monkeys, brine shrimp eggs which come to life in water. She has been gone for some time but anyway a box of presents arrives. The Sea-Monkey box illustration shows a papa Seamonkey smoking a pipe and reclining in front of the TV, the mama shrimp in an apron, smiling and holding a fry pan, the baby Sea-Monkeys riding bikes and wearing baseball caps backward.

Your dad fills a fishbowl and empties the Sea-Monkeys in. He moves slowly, without faith. After a few hours the pink specks come to life, propelling themselves in minute, brainless bursts. *Ambitious little sons of bitches,* is what your dad says then. *Look at those idiot things. What do they have, a bus to catch? Just look at them go.*

Share

Iт's тне раіn pills that I like.

People in other cultures know. Native Americans, say. That it isn't always a bad thing to want to leave one's boring own head. That there's nothing weird about wanting to exist, briefly, on another mental plane without worries. That's why people drink, right? That's why they smoke marijuana. And then there are athletes, who swear by the endorphins. Buddhists who swear by the practice of yoga.

But for me it is pain pills.

I love all of them. I love the whites, I love the blues. I love plain codeine. I love Canadian 2-2-2s.

Know that I am nearly fifty, and have a big butt and live in a cul-de-sac. Know that each spring I squander forty or fifty bucks on pansies, and fill the front yard with them, with their flimsy pathetic petals, and that even as I'm planting them I hate the way I look but cannot seem to see clear to a better option. Know that my walls are off-white and my life orderly, and that I use sheet-stays at all four corners of each of the beds in our home, and also I truly love Oprah. I watch her every day.

My husband works in construction. He's a general contractor, which is nice for him to not actually have to heft the sheetrock himself, but then again it's a stressful job because of the way he has to count on subcontractors who, often as not, blow him off or come up with flimsy excuses. We've been married since right after high school. I don't know, maybe that's part of it. Neither of us really experimented with much. I've only ever tried a joint once in my whole life, and then I coughed my head off. And I don't drink at all, and Ray only drinks Coors Lite. We've tried to set a good example for our daughter. Her name's Crissy, and she just moved to Laramie to go to college.

So the house is so quiet now. And when it gets too quiet my heart races, and then I feel tremendous sadness, and know that even if I go to sit on the front porch it might be hours before I even see anyone go past. And even then, except for the occasional neighbor who's lived on our block as long as we have—thirty years almost—well, people don't really want to stop and talk. And I can't think what to say anyway. I want so much to do it sometimes, because all the time and especially since Crissy left I feel, I don't know, just so old and done with what used to matter. It's probably just menopause. But there's so much I want to say, so much I want to do. And I just never seem to know how to reach out. I don't know how to make friends, I don't know how to get past the superficial stuff. Everybody just mostly seems too busy.

But back to the pills. I was twenty the first time I got them, after Crissy was delivered by emergency C-section and I don't think I knew what hit me for about the first week after her birth. Ray has me on videotape, propped up on the puny white hospital pillows with my beautiful beautiful baby right against my chest. And I think it's funny even now, the way I kept scratching my nose and my arms. I was on a morphine drip, you see. I thought my joy, my *ecstasy* really, was from the baby, and a whole lot of it was. But what I didn't know was how the morphine went into my brain and revealed my secret garden, and threw open the gate to that sunny, green place. It smelled of heavy, ripe tomatoes on the vine, and lavender and milky pink roses, and in this place everyone, every single nurse coming and going, was someone I loved, *loved*. And all that beauty made me sentimental, and everything made me cry. I thought everything, everything was beautiful. I loved the sound of the carts being wheeled around outside my door. I loved the small trays of adequate food, and the handicap bar next to the toilet, which was cool and chrome and courteous. I loved the nurses. I loved that I had everything I needed right there, and that I was the exact center and focal point of this particular hospital room, room 631, and above all, above all, I loved that baby. I love that baby.

So you see, when the surgery happened, I got opened up on so many levels. On so many! I just sort of expanded, if that doesn't sound too weird, in all directions. I can see that it was partly because I was high as a kite. But that didn't matter to me then, and it hasn't mattered the ten or twelve times that I've had a pain pill prescription since. I've had surgeries since then on both knees, and also had my deviated septum fixed, which was just a great idea all around since it meant that finally Ray and I could sleep in the same bed again.

Before that I'd snored like Fred Flintstone. And I've had heel spurs, and several abscessed teeth. It's funny, but as I get older I notice that the doctors are more liberal with the pain medication. In my twenties, as Crissy was growing up, they'd always ask questions like had I ever been treated for any sort of substance abuse, and had I ever done things like stockpile (!) drugs. I mean, really weird questions! But then by the time I was in my forties, I don't know, the doctors didn't seem to care at all. The last few years, they've been scribbling Lortab prescriptions right and left.

And I have to say, I love this.

I just really wonder sometimes, in the rocker on my front porch and thinking about Crissy and wondering where Ray stopped for lunch, all that, what other people my age do. The ones like me. The harmless-looking ones who hose off their driveways every day. I know other people must have secrets, like the way I love Lortab is mine. I know they probably do things they're not really supposed to enjoy. I don't know what, and I mean I don't like to think too hard, since probably some of those things have to do with sex. But I just wonder in what other ways people let themselves off the hook to relax. I hope it's not really bad things. I hope it's nothing that hurts anyone else. And then I wonder again why it is that humans have such a need to get out of our own heads, to alter reality as we all know it. I wonder why I need little white or blue pills in order to feel one with the world.

Possibly it is because otherwise I am not a spiritual person.

I mean sure, now and again we go to church. We're Lutherans. And that's okay. That helps, I like it well enough. But it only lasts as long as the service lasts, just like when I watch Oprah all of my feelings about how to resolve my problems and work off my big butt and heal the rift between myself and my brother, who I haven't talked to in years, go out the window. I mean well, but as soon as I turn off the TV I'm back in my real life. At least the effects of the pain pills last longer. I mean: one prescription basically equals a month of peaceful brain and deep love for my fellow man. That seems like a pretty darned good deal.

I like to bite them in half. I like to go and stand in the mirror and see myself then, a woman with frizzy blonde hair with half a pill on her tongue. I like to watch myself wash them down. I like then to put down the toilet seat and realize how, within the hour, I'll feel happy and whole. I like to think about what I'll do that afternoon after I've taken the half a pill, because frankly, they make me so happy that anything and everything sounds good. I can weed the flower bed or call friends or visit the old lady across the street because finally, for a few hours at least, I'm not lonely. Finally I'm at one with the universe.

And I like—oh, you'll think this is so silly it's funny. Like a cooped-up housewife's very own Easter egg hunt.

You'll laugh, but sometimes I can hardly wait for Ray to leave so that I can do this. Sometimes when I get a fresh prescription, like the last time when I had a tooth pulled, well, just to have a little fun I went into my sewing room, which is Crissy's old bedroom and which is packed full of stuff. I haven't used that sewing machine in probably ten years. And then there's all of Crissy's stuff in boxes. There's so much crap in there and it's such a small room that I practically can't even get the door open. So the reason I do this is when I have a room, like this one, that really needs to be tackled and organized and dealt with.

What I do is, I open the bottle. I dump some of the pills onto my palm, and break a few in half with my teeth. Then I throw about five of the pills out across the room, where they disappear between the stacked-up boxes and all the crap and books. It can't be too many because then I tend to find them all at once and it takes away all the fun. But then I have my work cut out for me! I usually spend the next few weeks clearing it out. I can't even tell you how much fun this is. See how dumb it sounds? But how can I explain? I get up, and fry Ray some bacon and do pancakes on the griddle. We have Sanka and breakfast out on the sun porch, and then he goes to work while I clean up the breakfast dishes. Then I return calls, and maybe polish the dining room table, and feed the cat. Suddenly my day, which would've been as dull and calm as the last, has *anticipation* in it. Suddenly there's something to look forward to: tackling a boring project that I've been putting off for years, because I will find on the floor or maybe fallen into the boxes or even once in the toe of a boot, the tiny white submarine shapes which give me such pleasure and an open heart. I can live with anything then. I can clean anything then. I take even one pill, and for hours I'm filled with love.

Sometimes I even call Ray to come home for lunch and we crawl between the sheets and there's that happiness. I like to imagine myself then as different women, Joan of Arc, Michelle Pfeiffer, Pocahontas. Why, I don't know, I guess I just think of her as sexy. Ray loves these times, when he's my chief Powhatan.

If I find more than about three pills in any one given cleaning, I just toss them back out into an especially junky corner. And that gets me motivated to tackle it for the next time.

Sometimes I want to tell Ray. Because what does he keep from me? Naked ladies on the Internet, I know that much.

If you took a picture of our house from out in front, you wouldn't see anything weird. That I can promise you. You'd see the well-tended shrubs, you'd see the healthy soil I've been enriching for thirty years. And a black wrought-iron railing, and the wooden whirlygigs that Ray likes to make with his jigsaw on the weekends. They're ducks, with wings that spin in windy weather.

I guess I just want to know, do other people have these feelings? I want to know why, when I have this happy and well-tended life, when we have clothes and friends and food on the table, it is only the medicine that can make me feel spiritual. Or whole, or part of a gentle and peaceful human world. I want to know why that is.

It's been worse the last year, I'll admit that. The wanting it. Since Crissy left especially. I'm happy enough but there is something about having children. There is a point that comes when they are small, after you've had them a few years, where you realize that there is no real way of being whole or intact again. And that's the beauty of having them, I know that. But there was a day, an exact day I remember, when that knowledge hit me.

I was probably twenty-six. Crissy was four years old, and I'd just dropped her off at the preschool. And then I drove home so slowly, so slowly on our winding streets in our neighborhood near the golf course, and I stopped the car because there were ducks in the road, a green-headed male duck and his plain brown mate. Where we lived there were also quail, and because it was spring we were seeing a lot of them, and the quail always traveled in groups of six or eight with sometimes the little baby fluffs scuttling in a line between the grown-ups. The ducks crossed without hurry, and suddenly then I felt the giant sadness of being a human who had to think so much about things, who had to analyze and try to understand every day how they felt about things; and why it was, when it would be easier on our hearts finally, that we couldn't just live like the ducks, who waddled in front of cars and pecked at the cracked corn we tossed onto our front lawn and clambered into the children's wading pools some of the neighbors put out every spring.

When I got home I thought maybe it was just hormones. I brewed myself some PMS tea and went to sit on the front porch.

And I thought, sitting there, how I barely even knew the people in my neighborhood. How mostly we all just drove out of the neighborhood, going to stores, going to ATMs, and then drove back, opening our garages with the remote before we disappeared into our kitchens to think up something for dinner and watch our TVs. I'm not saying we don't have friends and family. We do. But I could see, as though I were seeing all the moments of my life on one single sheet of white paper, that now, as a mother, I was in the *receding* part of my life; and that probably most of the people on our block, who also have kids, knew this on some level too. Before Crissy, there had been much much less to lose. Before her I'd been ripe, with an undamaged body and an attitude. And now I could see that even if Ray and I got sick of each other there was no getting in my car and just driving away. I could see that finally she would go away from us, and that I would every second of every waking day for the rest of my life worry myself sick about her. I could see that there was no turning back. And also knew that because of her, my life was more beautiful and meaningful than it had ever been.

But what I couldn't see, and what I couldn't understand, was how I would endure it.

So I sat on that porch, and cried away the rest of the morning. It was the same terror I'd felt as a little girl, when I'd wake up in the middle of the night and think about how I was eventually going to have to die and that there was absolutely no getting off the planet any other way. Terrified because this was the deal. You got your joy, and you got your grief.

Finally I collected myself and went to pick up Crissy. She was the most beautiful little girl. She had gold bangs that were always getting too long, and these enormous green eyes. Ray's.

Motherhood was a season: that's what I was seeing. You know how it is, when every time in your life feels like the present? Day in day out. And then things change, people move away or you change jobs or finish school, and suddenly realize that what you have, what you had, is *historical.* That things are different. I know it's the way it is; I'm a pragmatic person. Ray tells me that. When our parakeets died, one after another I wrapped them in paper towels and stuffed them into a plastic bag and dropped them into the garbage cans. I'm not usually a dweller, or a sulker, and I don't even think I'm all that sentimental.

All the same, motherhood sort of knocked me on my butt.

As Crissy got older, things stopped feeling so desperate—I could actually sleep at night, even when she went out on dates—but I could never shake what felt to me like that first crucial realization, that it was Crissy who all through those years had given my life meaning. That my own personality got put on the back burner, for the first ten years at least; and that nurturing her and making sure she was going to survive, *survive*, was pretty much what my whole life was about. And that this meant continued vigilance; and meant that in those early years especially I could almost never relax; and that the times that felt absolutely right, absolutely right in the universe, were when I could see meaning in my world. Where I could see the most cliché things, that life was fleeting and a gift and all that.

So I know that you may criticize me, when I tell you that pain pills had this same effect. I know you will think your things possibly about people who use drugs, and about the need for counseling and exercise and a balanced diet and self-help books and for the need for Ray and me to spend time as a couple, all that. And yet I will always allow myself this luxury, this Lortab, taken from the benevolent hand of any doctor who may offer. I see it in their eyes, when they ask me questions. I see it in their faces, when the white square of paper floats the distance between us. I see that we understand each other; that peyote buttons and the like are, after all, only for the most hallowed occasions, and not to be considered or taken lightly. I will think that they are for the moments not when my leg or my tooth or my back is in pain, but when it is my *heart*: that aches: that contracts; that knows itself small, and small and small and small, and terribly human.

But I am in pain.

That is what I think, before I swallow a pill, each and every time. On my hands and knees, in Crissy's old bedroom, so full of pointless artifacts now, my hands will slide into dark corners, funneling between cardboard boxes, and come up triumphant.

Please, let me tell you one last story. I am going to take you back to Crissy's birth. She was forty-eight hours old.

It was the middle of the night, and I was in pain. I'd been sliced, it seemed, from one hipbone to the other. They'd removed the morphine drip and now I was getting whatever it was, Percocet I think, every four to six hours. I had a nurse with a pinched face and a life that she hated.

All this came out later; for now, she was merely a nurse with a stringy salt-and-pepper bun and squeaky shoes.

I was fine at first. Four hours, then five, then six. I pushed the call button and waited fifteen, maybe twenty minutes. I thought maybe the nurse was busy with another patient. The hurting started low and wide, and then got sharper and deeper until even inhaling felt knifelike. I waited a few more minutes and pushed the button again and this time my nurse came in angry. "It hasn't been long enough," she said. The room was cast in grey. She lingered near the foot of the bed.

"But I hurt," I said. "I really hurt. It hurts to breathe."

At this, the nurse raised an eyebrow. As in, ain't that a bitch?

Then she left.

I waited. The sun came up, and by then my incision was on fire. The pain moved up my body in waves, and I realized that I'd been tensing the muscles in my shoulder—from the gut pain—and had managed to give myself a splitting headache. I pushed the call button and the same nurse reappeared. It hurt even to talk.

"I need medicine," I told her. "I've been sliced in half. I hurt."

"They're bringing you the baby to nurse," she told me. And a few minutes later they wheeled Crissy in. I asked another nurse about medication, and she told me she'd ask someone. Then they put Crissy against me and for a few minutes I concentrated on her; on my new baby's detail and perfection.

When she stirred against my chest, the pain took my breath away; and suddenly, without realizing it was going to happen, I threw up. The mean nurse watched all this calmly. She held out a pan for the vomit and flushed it down the toilet and then the other nurse took Crissy back to the nursery.

I was panting by now, and sweating badly. At one point I thought, idiotically, that I wanted a watch on my wrist. So that I could check—check to see how long it had been. The nurse with the bun watched me from the foot of the bed. She was morphing, through my misery, into something tremendously evil.

"Listen to me," I said. "You need to give me something. I'm not a wimp but I hurt like hell. This is a hospital. You're a nurse. You're supposed to *want* to help."

"It hasn't been long enough."

I started to cry then. The tears slid down in front of my ears but I knew it would hurt to wipe them away so I just waited for the tickling to subside. "It *has* been long enough. You know it has, it's been *hours*. Why are you doing this?"

"Don't think your life is going to be so great. And don't have a live-in boyfriend, since you can't trust them." Then she sat on the edge of my bed, perched herself gently, and spilled the beans. She worked most nights, she said. Her son was ten. She could not protect him. The boyfriend did things, horrible things to her son in his bed at night. She might have to kill them all, she told me, starting with the boyfriend. She said "I wish I was dead. I don't know what I'll do. What would you do?"

I shook my head. She was not an ugly woman. I'd been mistaken. Only that her face was putty-colored and her features unremarkable, that plus the grief that stooped her shoulders and lent sag lines around her mouth. In another life she could've been lovely, with crows' feet from smiling and highlights in her hair. "My son," she said again, and that was all.

Then she looked at me, and seemed for the first time to register my much punier predicament, and left and a few minutes later came back with the pills and a paper cup of water.

"You need to kick that sonofabitch out," I said.

But anyway, in her face was drowning. She couldn't kick him out. She had a job. She was here with me. She'd brought me eight Percocets, enough to practically kill me. "That's this dose plus your last one and a bonus for my being so mean," she said. "I am, I'm making it up to you."

She sat again on the edge of my bed and started to cry. Then she reached for my hand. She was wearing smiley-face earrings. Smiley-face earrings! She was still trying, do you see what I mean? Still getting out of bed. Still putting one foot in front of the other. Still paying her bills, and taking her son to school. And every moment that she was here—even now, with me—well, how could she go on? She was supposed to be protecting him. She was supposed to be saving his life.

I thought of her son, sitting in a classroom somewhere. Of her evil boyfriend, home slumped in front of the TV probably. Then I thought of a young girl in a factory somewhere like Thailand, assembling those depressing smiley-face earrings by the dozen.

So I shared. Of course I shared.

She took two blue pills from my palm and threw them back without water. Still clasping my hand, she went onto her knees next to my bedside and closed her eyes and bowed her head. After a minute I saw that she was *chewing* her Percocet, trying I guess to get it in her system as quick as she could. *Any port in a storm* came into my mind. It was what my mother said all through my own childhood to explain what people did for themselves, to themselves. Her tongue tunneled under her gums and she grimaced. She wasn't praying. She was just kneeling. With her eyes closed, with her fingers laced over her eyes.

The Broken
Children

Watching water boil: That was no longer innocent. Now I stood
watching it every time with my mouth ajar, before I slid the
pasta in; and the same with when my tub water was too hot or
anytime, Jesus any of those times, water shooting too hot out of
the kitchen tap, or when I poured boiling water off small red
potatoes, et cetera, and I couldn't think of anything then but
the boy and his friends, fallen. They were in Yellowstone. It
was the end of summer. They'd worked the last day at the
lodge, and packed up the car and intended to go for one last
soak before driving home in time to start college the following
day. That was when they were still three. Two boys and a girl.
It had happened so suddenly, so terribly, there on the dark
trail. They meant to hop over. They thought it was a stream, so
bright there in moonlight. And so they'd jumped.

One of the boys' mothers was my friend. They said their
names on TV, and showed the three teenagers' photos. I'd

frozen in my tracks before the TV and yelled: *Elsie, shut the fuck, fuck up!* at the biggest dog, who was loudly licking and snuffling at her backside. Then I sat on the couch and listened, and flipped through the other channels where they were telling the story and showing the pictures again and again, and there was nothing for it but to keep shaking my head, because it really just was not possible.

How could she survive it, the mother? And the dad and the sister. How could they live? *We all just sleep together in the big bed now*, the mortally wounded son's mother told me in the stark hallway. *All just in the big—* her voice broke. They were in the hospital because they were always in the hospital. Since it happened, since the boy had fallen in, well, they lived there now. It was a living. It was a life. There were Cup-a-Soups and a Coke machine and a telephone and even an *ottoman*, in the waiting room, and there were magazines fanned out by some hospital worker, some janitor instinctively fanning them to make all the families of burn victims feel right at home. There were visitors, all the time people in the hall waiting, waiting for an update, the boys were in critical condition, every moment their lives hung in the balance, there was nothing for it but to wait. What the family did sometimes was use the back entrance. They stood weeping in the elevator next to carts loaded with janitorial supplies and hospital food, more hospital employees—there were so many of them!—trying to give them privacy, watching for their floor button to light up, whistling the softest and most innocuous of tunes while the victim's family huddled. And then the three of them trying to pull themselves together, step out and correct their faces so that the boy, the beloved burned boy, if he came out of it, would see instead their happy shining faces full of hope. Would see instead their joy and love. *They couldn't cry all the time.* They would think that, sometimes, but it did no good. They cried endlessly, they cried whole rivers trying to bring him back, trying to bring that day back, and then that night, and then the moment, when the most gorgeous and treasured boy, god he was gorgeous, he was *luminous,* did the world understand that? He was *eighteen.* When the treasured boy had gone walking with his two closest chums, there were hot pools, it was a national park in all its majesty, the steaming pools and boiling rivulets everywhere, everywhere, and they were just going to hop over. I mean in the moonlight it was a fucking *trickle.* A *seep.* A seep to leap. They were walking arm in arm. They were in love. They had everything, everything. The girl had a cream-colored sweater tied over her jeans. They were just walking. Then they were just hopping. And for that moment the air held them in a bar of chilly moonlight, they had been doing a Laverne and Shirley thing right before it happened, arm in arm: *schlemiel, schlemazel, Hassenpfeffer Incorporated*—and then they dropped.

The girl went under. She was so small, and her sweater popped off and bubbled forth while the boys, jesus, they looked supernatural now, arching and thrashing, starfish, in boiling water. You could see it on the news later: their footprints on the bottom, left there forever beneath hundred-and-eighty-degree water, the water so clear it looked ice cold, really, like a martini, I mean you could see right through, it made no sense, there was no explanation.

The boys: they were stronger, their heads stayed up, somehow they clawed out, the skin already bubbling off, god help them, god help them, they found a cold pool, their screams led their friends, who hauled forth the girl, who hauled forth the boys, who carried their poached ruined bodies half a mile downhill, the girl came to and she was a goner, she knew that much, she moaned and begged to be put back. Just put back. The footprints on channel four. The camera zooming in, panning back, going in yet again for a closeup and for a moment even the newscaster's voice faltered, stopped. He was there with square glasses and his mouth ajar, just staring at the picture like the rest of us. You could see toe marks where their sneakers dug in some crazy fried-egg dance. You could see a quiet of trees beyond.

I felt like such a rubbernecker, looking in. I think we all did. And yet they were kind, the whole family was kind, we were friends and all trying to help, all trying to sit in the hospital hallway with a notebook and answer questions, which we were called *point persons*, and when you were a point person you went and sat for two hours and thought about all the useful things you might've brought, flowers maybe, maybe Cokes for the family, or maybe a *cake*: that occurred to me once, insanely, *maybe I should've brought a cake.* The other boy's family came and went, that mother turned inward in her grief, always weeping, moving mechanically back and forth between her son's room and the elevator. While two walls over the boys spasmed day in and day out with breathing tubes, their bodies swaddled in white gauze, somehow they reminded me of Easter chicks, I felt funny even seeing them because, you know, I was the mom's friend, how I adored the mother, but I'd met her son only one time and how would I like it, I tried to think, how would I like it if some whole freaking parade of strangers had to peek in on *me* if *I* ever had to lay there in some coma, the morphine cranked to eleven and still they suffered, jesus their spasms, their spasms and ragged breathing, you wanted to touch them and couldn't, couldn't, and anyway he didn't even know me, what kind of a freak was I, thinking I could help bring him back from the dead? By being a—a *point person,* was that it, was that somehow going to help? Me in the hallway with my pointless point-person notebook? When what I wanted always was to see my friend, his mother, and even when I did see her anyway I'd just cry, I was no help, I was supposed to be offering moral support and at the first sign of grief I folded, too, I let the poor exhausted burned boy's mother hold *me,* I couldn't think of one single goddamned uplifting thing to say. I was *just plain mad.* I was mad at—at *Christians,* I was mad at anyone for thinking there could be a God, if he was going to let this kind of ludicrous thing happen, and then I was mad at all the hospital employees because why did they have to all wear their stupid white shoes and just look *sorry sorry sorry,* I was mad at myself for getting snot all over my friend's shirt, mad at myself when she led me, we were clinging and crying like shriveled old Polish ladies, back to her demolished son's hospital bed. And then seeing him—rubbernecker that I was—and then thinking more foolish things, I couldn't stop thinking about them, I couldn't stop thinking about all the ways in all those years she'd protected him, lovely luminous boy, there were vaccinations, there were bike helmets and shinguards and car seats and then booster seats and rules, *look right and then left before crossing,* there were dental caries and bunk beds to worry about, and teenagers speeding through school zones to worry about, there were the cars in fact speeding through her own neighborhood that the mother had tossed things after, once a garden trowel and another time a *whole actual shovel,* did they know she had children here to protect, was it rocket science, was it, just to slow the fuck down? There were jungle gyms to worry about him dangling from, and poisons under the sink, there were child molesters and steak knives and more recently the hantavirus. And then for it to come to this. To the boy, tubed, opposite photos of his family and an important sign he'd crayoned to his family, at age five, on some occasion: *I'me here. Stay calm.*

I-mee, his mom pronounced, over his bed. *We put this stuff up so it's the first thing he'll see when he wakes up. And then know, know how very beloved*—she stopped, shook her head.

And then, what could we both do but look over at him? If you weren't already a wreck—well, for Christ's sake. I am telling you now—oh, what am I telling you? Do you know how they suffered? Do you know that the girl died? Do you know that the other boy, also beautiful, also barely pulled through? Do you know that a local newspaper, some cheap-ass-piece-of-shit loser-ass asshole newspaper, actually printed a crappy story— a *joke*—they thought it was a *joke*—called Look Before You Leap? Ha ha! So funny, get it? That's a good one! So subtle! I wanted to show them the boys, drag them by their crappy-ass threadbare lapels and make them stand over both those hospital beds. I wanted to show them the little sister, her narrow shoulders, her glance going sideways all the time now, sleeping *all the time in the big bed* with her parents, creeping past the older brother's empty room at night on her way to the bathroom. She was so small, when I saw her there in the hospital hallway, she pushed her hair behind her ears and tried to make sense of it aloud, tried to be mature: *I'm having sort of a hard time in school, just with everything.* And when were the angels going to come? When would they alight beside each boy's bed?

The burned girl lasted only a few hours at the hospital. Her parents were on the road somewhere, somewhere between

Washington and Utah, trying to get there in time, trying to get to their darling Sarah, but it was useless, her head had gone under, she was so small. It was my friend, the mom, who saw her into the next world, along with the burned boy's sister. They held her red, red hand and sang and talked. They stroked her thick dark hair through her murmurings, her thrashing. *How is Sarah?* one of the boys would ask a few days later, rising briefly from the depths to remember. The moms of both boys had it planned in case they were asked, because the doctors had specifically instructed: you can't give them any bad news right now, you can't, you can't, and so one of the mothers had planned to say: *Sarah is with some very good people.* But by then the boy had sunk again, and didn't hear.

Every day there were the baths. Here the skin was scrubbed, here the horrible burned skin rolled forth, here the boys screamed and cried and begged before they were returned to their rooms. There was the playing-card-sized patch of skin culled from each boy's neck and shipped to a clinic in Boston where it was stretched and watered and loved over like the most temperamental of house plants, and then returned in a cooler, the skin now the size of a sheet of paper, that was helpful, and placed tenderly over some portion of burn, and then this was done some hundred times more until finally finally finally each boy was more or less intact, they were sealed in anyway, more or less in their own skin anyway, and by now it had been three months, three months in critical! condi-tion, and by now their beds had been wheeled into the hallway so that they could see one another at least, their swaddled white arms propped so they could at least give the thumbs up.

They showed that on the evening news, too.

I thought then of the story I'd read as a kid, in some bible-story book in a dentist's office—where the kid in the hospital was sick, he was dying, so the nurse helped him prop up his arm with a pillow, the arm in a cast, the boy wearing a valiant bandage around his head, the boy ruggedly handsome and white and blond, to boot—and then his arm propped so that, when the angel came, she'd know which bed to go to. That one I blubbered over, waiting there in the dentist's office with my snotty-nosed sisters and all my cavities, I already had a whole mouthful of silver because I was a candy-chomping little slob who didn't brush often enough, I would never be heroic, I was a booger-eater, my hair was greasy, we were not churchgoers. Or like the boy in another book, called *The Littlest Angel*. And on page one the boy was in heaven, which was disturbing enough, and he was longing for a gift to give the Christ child, the gift of his special treasures such as rocks and frogs and a yo-yo which he kept under his bed back home, that's right, under his bed *back down on earth*, a room which perhaps by now had been shut up and entombed with the dead boy's things for all eternity. And some friendly angel went back down to earth and retrieved the box, if memory serves me, so that then the littlest angel could offer it to the Christ child, who then pronounced it, among the riches, among the bars of gold bullion and strands of jewels: *the greatest gift of all*. I was supposed to be caring about the Christ child, we all were, but how the littlest angel book worried me! And raised all sorts of questions! Like, how did the little boy die? Did he get run over on his bike? Was there tons of blood? Did his two front teeth get knocked out? Could he breathe in the coffin? Did he have shoes on when they buried him? Had his brothers and sisters pillaged his treasure box in the meantime? Did their family have a trampoline? Did his mom sit crying in his room every day? Had her hair turned solid white with grief? Did she wear it in a bun? Did people need to pee after they were dead? Above all, *who was going to get all his stuff*—his books and bike and Nintendo? How come, on page seven, how come when he scraped his knee it showed blood? Because wasn't your body supposed to be perfect in heaven? Because if he'd gotten smushed by a car on his bike down on earth, why was his body magically intact once he got there, but then suddenly he wound up with blood on his knee on page seven? And what had happened to the red girl, the one who died in the hot pool, after she died? I mean where did her personality go? Where did her great laugh wind up, and all the songs she knew, and also the jokes, and how could any of us do anything, we were point-people, we loved the boys, we loved the dead girl, we loved the suffering parents and brothers and sisters, we were appointed, we were *guardians,* we *prayed. I prayed,* endlessly, begging for mercy each time they wheeled a suffering boy by on the gurney on his way to yet another torturous bath, did they have to do that, did they really have to do that, exfoliate the burned skin, could any of us ever boil water again without thinking of them, or sit in a hot tub again, could any one of us ever think again of skin in the same way, as something protective and fragrant and browned by sun, and downy in places, and as something any rational person would take for granted? While the burned boys waited for their skin grafts to grow in that lab in Boston, they were covered temporarily in *donor skin,* and once without thinking I referred to it, to the burned boy's dad of all people, as *cadaver* skin. Yes, they'll use donor skin he said then, correcting me gently, there were right words for things, and wrong words, and right and wrong things to write in the point-person notebook, which was supposed to if possible give hourly updates on the boys' conditions. But there were long stretches, long hours where the boys merely hung in the balance with this or that infection, hours where their heart rates had dropped abruptly, and blood pressure too, and days of this; and so I took to taking poems to the hospital, took to copying them in the burned boy's notebook so that if and when he woke up he would at least have something to read. It wasn't the same as having comments to write about his condition, but still it was something, it was better than nothing.

I copied from a poem called *Blandeur:*

If it please God, let less happen.

And:

Unlean against our hearts.
Withdraw your grandeur from these parts.

Widen fissures to arable land; that was a line from the poem I left out.

My three-year-old son wants to know *why we don't say prayers,* like at Nana's house. Just don't talk during the prayer, okay? I say. Mommy and Daddy don't say the prayer but Nana and Papa do, so you have to be really really quiet. And say amen afterward.

Why don't we say it? He plays with his car seat straps, tempted to unfasten them but under threat of losing everything, all his toys, that's the agreement, *every last motherloving one of your toys will go to some other little kid, if you ever ever ever even once remotely unfasten that belt while the car is going.*

Because Mommy and Daddy don't believe in God.

Do *I* believe in God? He fidgets, plays with his seat belt, meets my eyes in the rearview mirror and drops his hands.

This one throws me. Mommy and Daddy don't believe in God because we believe in Mother Nature, I say.

Do *I* believe in Mother Nature?

Yes.

Does *Lulu* believe in Mother Nature? Lulu is the dog.

Yes. Listen, I'm serious, you can't blab during the prayer. This is important to me. So *no talking,* okay?

Okay. But around the dinner table, all the bowed heads start to get to him. He starts doing his gunfire noise, which is where I'm supposed to come in and say *say it don't spray it Bub.* I put one hand over his mouth and he freaks out, screams behind it, and when the prayer is over he says *that thing took way too long.*

Other people saw signs, other people had hope. The burned boy's parents saw eagles outside the hospital window, two together, soaring. And there were all the prayers that went up in those hospital corridors, and there were poems, and there was the moment when each of the boys opened his eyes for the first time, taking it all in—*I'me Here. Stay Calm.* And there were nurses and doctors, all pulling for them, and neighbors and friends like ripples on a pond, there were so many, so many who came, teenagers especially, the spirited friends with spiked hair and pierced eyebrows, with goatees and Patagonia fleece jackets, and the notes that got recorded hourly in the notebooks.

Once, when I could think of nothing else, I made a note in the point-person book: *the family has gone home to heat up some soup.* It was what I'd been told by the dad when he passed me in the hall, it was something, it mattered. There were right and wrong words. And one of the friends of the burned boy, a woman with spiky purple hair: she read my note aloud a few minutes later, pausing over the notebook: *the family has gone home to heat up some soup,* she read, mocking. *Who would write that?* she said. *What kind of an update is that?* And I was thinking, *soup is something. Soup is something.* Because they seem to me even now to have been the right words, the father keeping the heat turned to low, stirring and then lifting it from the burner, and spooning it for the wife and daughter into blue ceramic bowls, always now they had their guards up, there just wasn't any other way to put it, they took tepid showers and blew at their lifted spoons with care, they were putting their money now on plain old survival, they were thanking god or whom or whatever for everything these days, including canned soup with tiny cubes of red rubbery chicken, because any minute the hospital could call; any second the other shoe could drop. How they wanted to turn back the clock! How they wanted to go back, go back and flatten that majestic landscape, render it harmless as an old photograph! But two boys and a girl appeared. They moved up along one edge of the photograph and dropped toward the center, toward a small silvery fissure, and then they linked arms in the spirit of things and moved toward the jagged line, everything in color now.

Why did the cookie go to the hospital? my son asks. It's his first joke ever. The beautiful girl laughs at something one of the boys has said, pauses to tighten the sweater around her waist. My son has a tiny instant rehearsal under his breath before he delivers the punch line: *Because he felt crummy.* Then he goes back to his human body coloring book, working as usual in a monochromatic scheme, intestines and bones and skin all getting made what the Crayola wrapper calls *tangerine.* His own skin is so milky, so perfect. I can't imagine it happening to him. I keep staring, catching flies, dumbstruck at the possibilities: earthquake, car wreck, burning.

Do you think I'm funny? he says. He's still practicing for life. The dead girl, Sarah, had worked in a preschool. My friend's son had written home from Yellowstone the day it happened: *I think I can imagine myself here the rest of my life, working concessions, being the jolly old ice cream man,* the letter went. I think of perverts, I think of the unfriendly majesty of geysers.

You're a hoot, I say. A crackup. There are broken places everywhere across the planet. My son loves shouting out across gullies: *Hello? Are you fat or skinny? Do you have a lot of toys?* These are the important questions. He listens for the sound of his own voice, the thin voice of a mocking ghost boy, receding: *inny inny inny? oys oys oys?* it goes.

I hand him his sippy cup of apple juice. *Say thank you, Mother.*

Thank you Beautiful Mother.

Aww, you say all the right things.

I know, he says, and works at the juice for a minute before pausing to give me a complicated high five: *high five, on the side, in the hole: you got soul.*

The Gingerbread Boy

HIS DAD HAD TAKEN him to a restaurant.

Which was special; which was unusual; a real restaurant, with booths and ketchup bottles and plastic water glasses and a kids' menu with four crayons wrapped in a napkin alongside.

"Do you know what color restaurants use to make people get more hungry?" his dad asked.

"Orange?"

"Close," his dad said. His dad's name was Russell. "Good guess, you're a smart kid. It's red. Red makes people hungry."

"Why?" asked the boy.

"How should I know? It just does."

The boy, Adam, had just finished the kids' spaghetti-and-meatballs meal. He was ready to go but his dad was still eating and it was important not to make grown-ups crazy by bouncing on the seats and talking too much and spooning the ice out of his water glass, so Adam sat still. When his dad took a long swallow from his coffee, Adam watched and then practiced doing the same thing with his water. When he was a man he would drink coffee black like that and eat peppered beef jerky and be able to shoot a duck straight out of the sky. He'd be able to slam the air hockey puck as fast as his dad could do at the arcade. He would walk with the same long, lazy stride. He would get a Jeep and go up slickrock and drive through muddy rivers and then keep the red dirt right there on his truck for as long as he wanted.

"Have you thought anymore about Reno?" his dad asked him now.

The waitress came by, and Russell made a gesture to shush his son until she'd gone off again.

"Well?" Russell asked.

"I don't know. I guess."

"What do you mean, you guess? That's not a very straight answer. That's a crooked answer. You have to tell me because I can't read your mind."

"Where is Reno again?"

"Reno is Reno. Reno is in Nevada. Reno's where I'm gonna get you a horse."

"What does mom think?"

"Don't worry about what your mom thinks. Your mom has you and I have none. Does that sound fair? She has one and I have zero."

"But I mean, does she want me to go with you?"

"I said don't worry about your mom. I'm asking you. I'm asking for your opinion here. If you don't like Reno I'll bring you right back."

"I guess," the boy said. "I guess I like horses." He liked

black stallions best. If he went to Reno he could have a black stallion and ride it bareback across his own desert island. He could drink the milk from coconuts and make campfires and boogie-board every single day at the beach. Then his horse would gallop him away.

His dad yanked his water glass away sharply. "Stop hauling out your ice cubes. If I've told you once, I've told you a million times."

The boy and his mother had a game, because his mother wore contact lenses. What Adam would do was suck on a piece of ice until it was very small and curved. Then he'd cup it in his palm and say *my contact lens fell out! My contact lens fell out!* to make her laugh.

His mom, Brenda, had a smoky laugh that started out low and then rose and climbed up all around the room. Lots of times when other people heard her they would start to laugh too. But she couldn't keep a job and that was a problem. She would sleep too late in the mornings and then they would have to let her go. Or get the time wrong when she had to be there or miss the bus. But anyway, Adam didn't mind. Then she would walk him to school and they would goof around and look at things, like worms floating in the gutter after it rained, and his mom would point out which house or car was her favorite.

"Mom wants a hunter-green Jeep and a stereo with extra bass," he told his dad.

"Good luck," Russell said.

Then Adam remembered that his dad didn't like to hear about Brenda. "So how far is it to Reno?" he asked. "How do you get there?"

"Thirteen hours, tops," Russell said. He finished off his

coffee and leaned back and lit himself a cigarette. When Adam grew up, he would smoke cigarettes too. And maybe then he and his dad could go for a walk together down a dirt road where they could find arrowheads.

"What else did I tell you about Reno?" Russell said. "Did you put it in the memory bank?"

"I like horses. You said you might get me one."

"I know. You like black stallions like that little faggot in the movie."

"And you could get me one?"

"Is that the only reason you're going? What about me? We'll be buddies. Just you and me."

Lots of times, what Adam was going to get in the way of presents was exactly all he cared about. He couldn't help himself. And both of his parents knew and so they would try to compete, which was especially hard on his mom. Because they had so little money, she would compete with his dad's big and expensive presents by using her imagination. She'd paint him pictures, or buy toys from the thrift store and clean them up nicely. But a new toy was a new toy, and it wasn't just the stuff itself that Adam liked and wanted. It was the way it made him feel like a normal kid. Like at his dad's house, where if he printed out pictures from the computer he didn't have to worry about using up all the ink. If he dumped cereal into the bowl and then changed his mind he could put it straight into the trash instead of try to pour it back in the box. He didn't like how it felt when he was worrying about money. He believed secretly that children shouldn't have to worry about such things. And that they should be allowed to be noisy and wasteful and not worry about a mother's sad expression when the mail arrived or when she glanced at the gas gauge in their old car and then found a gas station and put only a few dollars' worth in instead of filling the tank.

"Would we ever come back?"

"Of course we could come back if you wanted! I already told you that. It would all depend. But remember I want us to leave, if you're going to come with me, day after tomorrow. So you gotta decide."

"What about my school?"

"I can teach you," his dad told him. "Some parents do that. It's called homeschooling. We just decide, like this week we're going to do math and next week spelling and you just do that. Only at home."

"Where?"

"At home I said."

"No, but I mean where would you do the work?"

"Wherever you do your homework, I guess. In front of the TV." Russell laughed at his own joke and stroked the tips of his moustache. "Anyway, remember, don't tell your mom about our potential Reno expedition. She'll just wig out and send the cops out after me. This is just between you and me, got it, pardner? Shake on it."

His dad dropped him at the curb. That was how it was. His mom would drop him off at the curb of his dad's house and watch until he got inside. And then at the end of the weekend it was the other way aound, like now.

They were having pigs-in-a-blanket for dinner. The boy slowed guiltily, remembering. He would have to eat anyway to keep from hurting her feelings even though he was still full from the spaghetti.

His mother was at the stove. She kissed him and then

looked closely. "I knew it," she said. "He does it on purpose is what he does. It's not your fault for eating but I at least hope you saved some room since I made these special today for us."

"I'm still hungry," Adam said.

"Well, go wash up. These are almost ready."

Adam played in the bathroom for a while. His dad had given him a bar of soap that had a small toy dinosaur inside that you could see. You had to wash and wash until finally the soap melted away and then you got the dinosaur.

"So come tell me about your weekend," his mom called.

He soaped thoughtfully, turning it over and over in his hands. He did this every time but still the soap looked just the same.

"We had fun," Adam said. Always it was a balancing act to let his mom know that his dad wasn't more fun than she was. Because she worried. That his dad, as she put it, would wine and dine him all weekend long and make it seem like that was real life, with trips to restaurants and arcades and bowling alleys and going out ATV riding. When really a real life was like the one they had. Where he got woken up too early each and every morning and then packed off to school, and then there was homework later and boring meals and too much TV. Adam knew that this was so, but still the end of the weekend was always a letdown.

"Like what'd you do?"

"Just stuff."

"Well did he take you up in the mountains again?"

This was a trick question. Adam soaped slowly, considering his answer. The mountains, which he knew from answering this question last time, were only a few miles from the state line of

Montana. And the reason this mattered was because Russell was forbidden to take Adam across the state line on account of his mom had custody. Lots of questions he got asked by his mom and dad were like this. They didn't really want to know whether he'd had fun, it seemed, as much as they wanted to know whether the other one was cheating or playing by the rules.

"No. We just played miniature golf. I got my ball all the way up into the hayloft of the little red barn."

"Did you win then?"

"No. Dad hit a ball all the way across the moat and got twenty-five points."

"Yep. Too bad he can't make a career out of his stellar performances at miniature golf."

"Dad has a career." Why did she have to pick on his dad? The thing was, he loved his mom so much but she was tired all the time.

"Finish up in there, okay?"

The dinosaur was where it always was. Frozen and clear and deep in the bar of soap and as far away as China. He would be fourteen before he ever got to the thing. He turned the tap from cold to hot and left the soap there in the sink long enough to get his hunting knife from his secret treasure box he kept under the bed. His mom didn't know about the knife but his dad had said every boy needed one, and this seemed true and right. He went back to the bathroom and turned off the tap. If there were horses in Reno he could maybe ride one every day to school. That would take away one boring thing, his ride in the noisy cold yellow school bus every morning. It would take away the walk to the bus stop with his mom, who insisted he hold her hand which he was too old for. But it was a highway and so she insisted.

And there was one feeling that had been bothering him for quite a while now. He could not think who to talk to about it. Usually if things made him sad, it was she he talked to. But more and more lately he'd had this feeling and he couldn't tell Russell because he might blab it back to his mother. And he couldn't tell Brenda because it would make her cry, oh Lordy how it would, and also because good sons didn't have feelings like he was having. He was pretty sure about that. Good sons loved their moms more than they loved anybody else. But what made it hard was how they had to struggle so much for things. Their house was too small and Brenda smoked too much, which made her clothes and also the carpets and couch stink of old cigarettes. His mom didn't get out of the house enough on account of her not having a job, and this meant she waited for him at the bus stop after school and of course again made the two of them hold hands on the walk back home. Even last year this had been all right. But he was too old for it now and she didn't even seem to see. And Adam thought that if his mom would just maybe find a way to make her hair shiny, or wear perfume or occasionally a necklace and high heels, it would be different. He wouldn't be having the feelings he was having now. He wouldn't go off with his dad on weekends and feel like a weight had been lifted, and he wouldn't spend the weekend being taken fun places by his dad and getting practically every meal from the drive-thru and staying up late to watch movies where men in sunglasses had guns and spoke into walkie-talkies and peeled out, leaving the cops in their dust.

He put the soap on the floor next to the tub and then stuck the knife in. One corner of the soap broke off this way, and so he did the next corner. But this time the soap flipped and the knife too, and suddenly he felt a hot flash of pain and heard himself make a noise and when he looked down he saw a deep red gash in his middle finger and deeper down, a gleam of white, and then his mother was in the doorway.

"What happened? What happened?" she cried, and snatched up a towel.

Adam shook his head. His hand throbbed and he wanted to cry but mostly he wanted her to leave, her voice so alarming and high. He thought that if she left he could fix things. He was dizzy and the things in the bathroom were right there but he couldn't seem to connect the things with what needed to be done. His knife, for instance: he needed to hide the knife before she got hold of it.

"Oh shit, oh shit, get in the car, get in the car," his mom was saying. She'd wrapped his hand but the blood was seeping darkly through. "Where did you get that, where did you get that thing?" his mother was saying. She scooped him up. "Did your goddamned dad give you that thing?"

"I was trying to get the dinosaur out." The knife was long and silver with a carved handle and it had a leather sheath. It was the knife from when his dad used to hunt deer. And it was Adam's most prized possession. His cut finger throbbed and he struggled to be put down. If he could get to the knife without her seeing—but he was dizzy and had to sit down fast on the toilet. He heard water running, and it sounded far away and he watched dumbly as she shut it off.

"Hold this," his mom said. "You hold it as tight as you can with the other hand until I can get you to the hospital. Oh shit oh shit oh shit." And now the knife was a goner. The knife was for skinning deer and it was from the olden days. His thoughts were coming all on top of each other and there was a metallic smell in the small bathroom, a sharp heated-up smell like the smell when Sparkie had had her kittens. He tried to stand but crashed into the sink instead. Maybe he would lose his finger and then not be able to hold a pencil anymore. Maybe he'd lopped it right off at the knuckle and he'd have to wear part of a fake finger for the rest of his life. He felt himself in his mom's arms, lifted and soon in cool air, and felt the car engine start. What state was Reno in? He'd forgotten. He opened his eyes there in the backseat so his mom would know he wasn't dead. He'd never seen her drive so fast! The trees whipped whipped whipped by.

"So, will you let me have my knife back?" Adam had three black stitches just above the middle knuckle of his finger. If he'd cut open his head the doctors would've had to sew big zigzag black stitches on his forehead like Frankenstein.

"You've got to be kidding me. After you practically just chopped off your whole finger?" His mom drove slowly. He watched the back of her head, the twist of yellowy hair. They'd given him medicine that made him feel fuzzy and tired and talkative. He knew better than to ask but he couldn't stop thinking of it, how if only he'd cut the soap when she was away from the house he'd still have the knife and how it was even more humiliating the way she'd caught him at it. Plus that he had passed out. A bigger kid wouldn't have fainted. And then his mom had carried him up to the emergency entrance in her arms, like he was a baby. And he would never be able to grow to be a man if she did these things. And all this was confusing because he could think all this and yet at the same time want her to pull the car over, and hold him and wipe his hair from his forehead and hum a soft tune. He unbuckled and slid forward and draped his good hand across her shoulder. His mother was his babyhood and his dad was something else.

"You're too young for such a knife," his mother said, and took one hand off the wheel to hold his.

"I'm eight."

"That's right."

"It's my favorite thing out of everything I own."

"Well, I'm sorry but you can kiss it good-bye."

"Please don't take it away." His head felt light and peculiar and floaty. And now he would have to explain to his dad about how the knife getting thrown away was his own fault. He would catch hell for it because if his dad had told him once he'd told him a million times, never let her see that thing or it's a goner. He withdrew his hand and sat back to study his wrapped one, which was like a mummy hand. That was cool. He liked mummies and especially the mummy on Scooby Doo, who always just turned out to be a guy wrapped in strips of white sheets and just dressed up like a mummy and trying to chase Shaggy and his buddies away so he could inherit the mansion.

"Are you going to tell dad?"

"He'll hear from me, let me tell you," his mother said, and craned her neck to shoot him a look that meant business. "You could've lost a finger."

"It's not dad's fault. It's my fault for getting it out when you could see it."

"What kind of an idiot would give their eight-year-old son such a thing? It is so his fault."

"It isn't."

"It is."

"No it isn't and you blame him for everything. And now you're going to take away my favorite thing."

"Well I'm sorry about that. But look at you, look what happened. The problem is he does these things, he tries to get even or top me or whatever his motivations are which I can't even begin to even guess—" and she went on and on for some time in this way, while Adam counted white cars out the window.

When they got home his mother went straight into the bathroom and snatched up the knife with its tooled leather pouch. "Don't," Adam said. "Please, Mom."

"Say good-bye. Then you need to lay down for a few minutes." She stalked to the kitchen and pulled a tray of blackened pigs-in-a-blanket from the oven. "Look at that," she said. "Ruined. We're just lucky the whole house didn't burn down."

"What are you going to do with it?"

"With what?"

"With my hunting knife." The boy's heart was full; he couldn't bear the thought. And if she took away the knife for good it would change everything between them. He watched it as she moved around the kitchen. Him and his dad and his knife were all connected and if she took that one part of things away, he would hate her.

"What do you think I'm going to do with it, Adam? I know it's one of your favorite things and I'm sorry but honest to God, what do you expect? How do you think I'm even going to pay for that little jaunt to the hospital? Huh?"

"Not one of my favorite things. My very favorite one."

"Jesus," his mother sighed. "Stay here. It's going."

He watched from the window as she crossed the parking

lot of their apartment complex and tossed it into the Dumpster. She looked jaunty; she looked pleased with herself. If he were a wizard he could magically halt the knife in its trajectory and send it speeding back toward the open window. His mother didn't look sorry at all and now he was going to catch it from his dad too, and it was all her fault for walking in on him when she had. And if she would leave him alone once in a while he would be able to accomplish more things, instead of always asking what was he doing and getting in his face and forbidding him to lock doors or have any privacy or life that didn't include her bossy, bulging face. "I hate you!" he yelled. But she was chatting with a neighbor and ignoring him.

In the old days his family had been all in one piece. Back then he'd had one single small bedroom with lots of posters taped to the wall and his Power Rangers sheets on the bed, and a driveway where he could lie on his stomach on his skateboard and go down. And a fridge with an ice-maker and satellite TV. His dad had a blue chair where you could kick with your heels and that part would pop up and then the whole chair would lay you back. His mom worked as a nurse at night. In the mornings her hair would still be pulled back tight from her face, which was unattractive, and sometimes she'd wear her white nurse shoes all over the kitchen. In the old days their house had been quiet, waiting always for some eruption. These usually came at twilight when Adam was out shooting hoops. Then the voices of other kids on the street would lapse slowly into darkness while the voices from the window of his own house grew louder. His mom and dad would be fighting then; and at this, Adam would make a basket one last time and then set out across the field next to his house, and only return when the house was quiet.

Nowadays it was nice to not have to listen to them fight anymore, but still and all his life felt wrong. For starters, things were in the wrong place. Before, for example, Adam had had a Power Rangers sheet to lie on and also one to bring up over his body when it was too hot for blankets. Now one of the sheets was at his mom's house and the other at his dad's, just like how his baseball was sometimes one place and his bat in the other, or the pants of his soccer uniform here but the shoes there. But then again he had two different and entirely separate bedrooms and how many kids could say that? was what his dad was forever pointing out.

But there was one thing he didn't have two of and that was the hunting knife. Adam stood at the window, watching his mother. She was talking with one of the single men who lived in the complex. She was flipping her hair back and smiling. Then another neighbor came out and heaved his own shiny green-black bag right up over the edge of the Dumpster. Now the knife had fallen, maybe, to the bottom, under all the pop cans and pizza boxes. "You fucker," Adam said to the neighbor. He was absolutely never under any circumstances allowed to say the f-word and so he tried it again: "You fucker," he said. Then he opened the window and yelled down at her. "I want my knife back!" Adam cried. "It was dad's and he gave it to me!"

His mother paused. She was laughing and touching the man's arm, and from her gestures Adam could see that she was telling him about the soap and the knife and their trip to the hospital. But she was putting a spin on it, making it seem almost funny from the looks of it, and so Adam yelled it again: "Give me back my knife!"

She gazed up at him. For a split second Adam saw a blankness in her face. He wanted suddenly, piercingly, to make her remember him; to make her see that she was trapped in this world as keenly as he, with a broken heart and no hope for the future and no life apart from the misery of this single evening. She was *his*. "What?" she called up, exasperated now, and the neighbor man slipped away.

His mother's face changed; the liveliness fell away, and some of the air seemed to go out of her body. Often when she talked to men she was like a bright, puffed-up bird, cocking her head as they spoke, watching them with a beady and keen interest. But always there were other women in their apartment complex who were better-looking than her; and always there was Adam himself who, when he sensed danger, could do exactly as he'd just done and remind his mother—either by tugging at her hand or acting bratty or making demands or calling down from their window—that he was the center, her reason for being.

"What?" his mom said, and stomped up the stairs and slammed into the apartment. He stayed at the window, staring out at the Dumpster. In a moment another neighbor would appear—a teenaged boy—and toss a broken patio chair up over the edge. Then an older woman, walking with a halting step, with a small white plastic bag of trash. Adam wanted to show his mom how it was; how sometimes the knife thrown end over end could land upright in the grass, and how the carved handle felt cool and weighty in his palm, making him a strong boy, a savage boy, someone brave, someone else. How just holding it could make him think of castles and soupy green moats thick with pythons and crocodiles. He tried to collect himself, tried to think of some way to reason with her, but when the words came out they were watery and trembled.

"I really, really, really, really, really want it back. Please. Mom. I'm begging you. I'll do anything."

"Want what back?"

"My knife, what else!"

"Adam: no. I'm sorry. Look at your hand, why don't you! Now listen, I need to talk to your dad. I'd like you to go have a rest in your room."

"Please don't tell him."

"Adam. Go." She lit a cigarette and blew the smoke carefully off to the side, waiting.

"Please just let me have one more chance."

"No."

"Just one more chance! I'm not a baby!"

"Go!"

"I hate you!" Adam cried. "I just love dad! I hate that I have to live with you and I hate our whole house!"

"Well, I don't like you that much right now, either."

It came to him suddenly that it was his hysteria, the way he yelled and flailed, that kept her from taking him seriously. He was not going to get his knife back. Not ever. That much was clear. And the way she stood calmly in her halter and shorts and casually smoking her cigarette was what made her seem so superior.

It infuriated him; he wanted to kick her shins and butt his head into her soft fat tummy and make her slide to the floor and sob. But he would have to beat her at her own game. And so instead of running to his room and slamming the door like always, like a baby, like a little boy with no control or money or manhood or independence or anything else, Adam faced her and kept his voice low and spoke meaningfully.

"You're such a loser," Adam said. "You can't even take care of us."

His mom's hand dropped, and her mouth opened a little. "You take that back now before I spank your butt."

"I mean it," Adam said. "It's not your fault that you're a loser but you are."

Then Adam went to his room.

He listened, and a few moments later she came in and stretched out next to him on the bed. There was terror in his body, and he tried to make his brain blank. He stared and stared at white bandage.

"How could you say such an awful thing?"

And it was as if now that he'd started it, he had to finish it.

"You can't get a job," he said. "You never wash your hair enough. You smoke cigarettes and stink up the whole entire house. You're an embarrassment."

"I should smack your face!" his mom said, astonished.

"Do what you will." Adam inspected the bandage up close. Maybe he would go as a mummy for Halloween. There was a trembling deep inside himself, and his throat felt tight and dry. He wanted badly to swallow, but there in the quiet terrible of the room he knew that she'd hear the gulp and know that he was sorry and guilty and only a small boy after all. So Adam held still. If she was sorry enough maybe she would retrieve the knife. If she loved him she would go and get it and they would never have to speak of this again and she would know, though he wouldn't have to say it, how sorry he was.

But he had said things that couldn't be taken back.

After a minute, he felt her sit up.

"Well," his mom said. "So." Her voice was mocking and

chilly. He understood that now they were in a new place. She rose and moved about the room, tossing clothes into his laundry hamper, pushing things into his closet with her foot and shutting the door hard. She was someone else's mother now.

When Adam woke up the next morning his room was warm and bright. He went to the kitchen and saw by the clock that it was ten-twenty in the morning; his mom hadn't bothered to wake him for school and there was a note on the kitchen table: *went to the market, call me on my cell if you need anything.* From her note and from the way she hadn't written his name or signed "love" at the end, he could tell that she was still mad. He picked up the phone and called his dad.

"That is one serious bummer about my knife," Russell said.

"I'm sorry. I hate her."

"Oh, it wasn't your fault. You were just being a kid. I used to do that sort of shit all the time. I used to play with matches. One time I went over to my friend's house and I wound up accidentally setting their whole newspaper recycling pile on fire. So don't sweat it too much. How's your hand?"

"It's no big deal. But I'm not ever going to speak to mom again until she lets me have my knife back."

"That'll be a cold day in hell. She's stubborn like a pregnant mule is stubborn. Stitches, huh? How many?"

"Three."

"You'll have to show me. Where's your mom at, anyways?"

"I don't know and I don't care."

Russell laughed. "Well well. Aren't you the tough guy."

"She treats me like I'm a baby."

"She does coddle you. You're her only one, so. That's why."

"Can you come help me get it?"

"Get what?"

"Your knife. She just put it in the Dumpster. We could just climb in."

"Listen, I'll get you another knife. A better one. Have you thought about what we talked about? The Reno idea?"

"Yes."

"And?"

"I don't know."

"Well do you want to come or what? I was thinking about it some more last night. I was thinking what would be cool is, I could get some of those rice paper screens, you know like along the lines of those kinds you see at the swap meet. I could buy a whole bunch of them and then set them up all over our room at angles to each other and thereby create a rice paper maze. Then you'd have your very own maze in your room. For when other kids came over. Wouldn't that be so cool?"

"Like, right in my bedroom? How would they fit?"

"My new house is going to be huge. I've already decided. Or whatever, we could even take out a wall if we had to. Or get you a fireman's pole, excuse my French fire person's pole, you could slide down every morning at breakfast. I always wanted a fireman's pole when I was a kid."

"What about when they're supposed to take my stitches out?"

"How's about I just do it? Nah, kiddin'. But there's doctors in Reno. Not like we're going to the North Pole."

"Are you really going to get me another one? Another knife?" Sometimes Adam's dad made promises. Then he drank too many beers and forgot about them, or got angry and yelled or fell asleep.

"Of course! A huge one if you want. With a carved ebony handle. Look, just say you want to go. That's all I need to hear. I'll work it out with your mom. But you have to help. You have to lay low and cooperate. You need to pack a few things, like maybe just in with your school stuff in your backpack, and then I'll pick you up after school tomorrow. How's that sound?"

"Won't mom be mad?'

"Quit hiding in your mama's skirts," Russell said. "You're practically nine. Are you in?"

Adam paused. He could hear what he thought were his mom's footsteps on the stairs. Soon she'd be back and doing the same things she did every day. She'd fix him mac 'n' cheese and watch her soap operas and they'd be stuck here together, in the small apartment without air conditioning, for the rest of their lives. And if he went with his dad it would only be for a few weeks at most and then he could come home and show her that he could function perfectly beautifully without her, without her meddling and throwing out his things and acting all the time like she was the boss of him. He was not supposed to talk to his dad behind her back, and this was another thing that suddenly made her seem even more wicked. He was almost nine, which was almost ten, which was close to being a teenager, yet still he was not allowed to talk to his own dad without her permission.

He'd been watching the Dumpster all morning, and now a fat man struggled up the stairs from his basement unit with three heavy garbage bags. He hauled them slowly, one by one, before finally getting them up over the edge and into the Dumpster. By now the leather sheath would be stained with orange juice or sour milk so that even if they did fish it out it would be for the rest of his life stinky and sticky and ruined.

"Well?" Russell said. "I ain't got all day."
"I'm in."

He didn't want to go with his dad; not really. Well, part of
him did. The part of him that wanted to impress Russell
and let Russell know that his son was almost a man now,
and smart in spite of how he'd about lopped off his own
finger, plus he liked the idea of an adventure as much as
anyone. They could drive fast on the highway and his dad
would be able to tell him things and they could stay up
late watching the kinds of TV shows that he wasn't
allowed to watch at home.

Then there was what he'd said to his mom. It would've
been different maybe if after he'd said it she'd cried and said
she was sorry about the knife. If maybe she'd forgiven him for
saying she was a loser. Instead she'd let him fall asleep
without kissing him goodnight, and then left her chilly note
about going to the market and let him miss school even
though he had a spelling test today, and if that wasn't being a
loser mother than what was?

Adam poured milk over his Cheerios and watched cartoons
while he ate. His mom came home and glanced in at him and
said shortly, "Does your hand hurt? Do you need any medicine?" and then when he shook his head no she'd shrugged a
little, like she didn't much care what his answer was, and
turned on her heel and put away all the groceries with a slam
before going to her room. And would a good mother act this
way? He drank the milk at the bottom of the bowl. One time
Russell had told Adam that his mom was good at guilt trips,
and Adam supposed that that's what this was. It gave him
something important to tell his dad. Even still, part of him

wished that he could make himself just go to her room and say he was sorry and that she was a great mother after all and then maybe they could go thrift-shopping together, something they both enjoyed. But one thing, he should pack up his backpack for the following day while she was shut in her room. While he had the chance. Before long she'd be back in his business, checking his backpack to make sure he hadn't forgotten his homework or book money and the note of excuse she'd written for his teacher, Ms. Atkinson.

He packed and then played tetherball in the front yard until nightfall. His mom had dinner waiting when he came inside, though she hadn't called him in. She left him to eat alone, and he heard her sniffling in the bathroom. When she finally reappeared to wash the dishes her eyes were pink and puffy. But it was like they were just going back and forth. He'd be ready to say sorry and then she'd reappear and catch him off guard, or she'd look sad and like she was about to say something and right then he'd slide off the chair and deposit his dishes in the sink and quietly leave.

He watched TV for a while and then got himself ready for bed and lay in the dark with his back to the door.

"You really hurt my feelings last night with what you said," his mom said a few minutes later from the doorway. "I know you just said it to hurt me, but still."

Maybe it was because he was trying to keep his nerve for what was going to happen the next day, when he got in his dad's car after school and then drove away with him to Reno. But he could feel that he was about to cry and so Adam concentrated on running his finger around and around the cool black bead of his rubber T-Rex's eyeball. Then he touched the claws to his tongue, one by one.

"Are you listening? I miss you. I know you miss me too."

"I *don't*," Adam said. He didn't even care so much anymore about the knife. But somehow he'd made a place in his brain where he could go with his dad to Reno and have a reason, and not feel bad. And she was tugging at these threads, trying to unravel things. If he went with his dad he'd have his own whole new bedroom, Russell had said, with his own large-screen television and cable hookup. It wasn't as if they'd be gone forever. It would just be for a vacation for a few weeks and then if he wanted to come home he could. And in the meanwhile his mom could have some time to herself. She worried so much these days that she had circles under her eyes.

"Why do you want to stay mad?" his mom asked.

"I don't."

"Well, you're sure dug in."

"Well, you're the one who threw away my knife."

"Yes. Aren't I a terrible mother?"

It was a test. He felt the mocking, the way she dared him to say it again.

"I didn't say you were terrible," Adam said carefully. "I just think maybe dad could do a better job sometimes."

"You think?" His mom said, and laughed a little. "Listen and I'm sorry again about the knife. I really am. But as long as I'm your mother, as long as I have custody, your boyhood will be knife-free. That's just the way it is, Adam."

He could feel that she was going to kiss him goodnight. He wanted to turn and have her hold him and say he was sorry. He wanted to have her lemony hair make curtains on either side of his face, like when he was a smaller boy, and then she would kiss the tip of his nose and they would make cross-eyes at each other. But if he relented and let her cuddle him then it would put things right back to the old boring way. So when she kissed his cheek Adam yanked away and said, "Your *breath* stinks." And she stood for a long moment next to his bedside, smelling in fact of some flowery hand lotion, before she went away.

"Well?" Russell said. "So what'd you bring?"

Adam unzipped his backpack and emptied it on the seat between them. He hadn't been able to think what to pack. He'd never moved to another state before. There were his schoolbooks and a Ziploc baggie with pens, and his pajama bottoms and his toothbrush and a roll of dimes and his T-Rex and a pair of sneakers and that was all.

"Shit," Russell said, and rubbed Adam's hair playfully. "What are you planning to wear? We'll have to buy you a whole new wardrobe. But I guess you couldn't pack too much, right? Or your mom would've been suspicious. Anyways, who cares, as I am totally psyched about Reno," Russell said. "The economy's *booming* there. Unlike here. I'm thinking we can get an apartment first and then look around for a house once we have some money saved up."

"Have you told mom yet that I'm with you?"

"Not yet. Gotta get over that state line, first. What's bugging you? You look all bugged about something. I can get you another knife you know. How's your finger, by the way? It hurt much?"

"It's okay." Adam stared out at the highway. It was twilight, and by now his mom would be frantic. He wasn't sure he wanted to be going to Reno anymore, but he'd made his bed and now he would have to sleep in it. He had stood right on his two feet and said what he'd said to her face, that she was a loser, and then he'd told her that her she stunk. There was no way to take it back; and anyway the part of him that wanted to cry, the part of him that thought the empty highway looked almost unbearably lonely, was the baby part of him.

"Mom's going to freak out," Adam said. "The bus always gets there at three-thirty and she's right there waiting. She makes me hold her hand."

"No shit?" Russell said. "How *embarrassing*. With your friends watching and everything?"

"Yep."

"Well. I won't be doing that shit in your new life, I guarantee it. You're too old for that. Anyway what I'm thinking is, we get there, we set up shop or household so to speak, than when I get enough money socked away we can get a house with some property out back and then we'll get you that horse."

"I told mom she smelled bad last night."

"You what?"

"Told her she stunk."

"Why'd you do that?"

"I was just still mad I guess."

"Well, you shouldn't talk to your mother that way."

"I know. When we get to Reno I might want to call and say sorry."

"Well, we'll see about that. She could trace the number and then my ass would be grass. We'll lay low for a while, get established, then we can talk about contacting your mom."

"She probably fell asleep at the bus stop waiting for me." He knew his dad didn't like to hear about Brenda; Adam did know that much. But he kept thinking about her there at the bus stop. It was dark and he wouldn't be surprised if she was still standing there waiting. Waiting and weeping, weeping and waiting.

"Wait, wait. Back up. Back up. Instant rewind. At the bus stop? You told her you were going to a friend's house, right? That was part of our little agreement."

"Oh crap," Adam said.

"Did you *forget?*"

"She'll just think I'm at Ben's house."

"You *forgot?* How could you forget that part of it? She's going to sic the cops on my ass!"

"I'm sorry, Dad. Anyway we can just tell her it was just for a couple of days. So she could cool off."

"Tell that to the lawyer, mister attorney boy. Shit." His dad used his forearms to steer while he opened a bag of Cheetos. "You shouldn't say stuff like that. She gave you the gift of life. And especially now that she's having a hard time with the whole job-hunt situation thing, she's like a fragile flower, if not such a fragrant one. You ought to lay off."

"I didn't mean it. I was just mad about the knife." His throat tightened, and he tried to push away the smell and feel of her next to him on his bed, her cool hands and low voice.

"I'll get you another knife. I'll get you a better knife. We hit a few pawn shops, I'll bet we can find you a really cool one. But first I gotta line me up something in the way of producing an income. I figure after I get you set up in school on Monday I can hit the pavement. I'll get something. I have tons of experience."

"I thought you said I didn't have to go to school."

"Huh? Whose dad was that? Every kid has to go to school."

"I thought you said I could do school at home." Adam

helped himself to the Cheetos and when he took a swig of his dad's beer, which he kept disguised in a Dr Pepper can, Russell laughed.

"Maybe we can try that next year. I have to brush up on some of my subjects first. But anyway, I haven't really decided. It might actually be a problem, trying to get you enrolled. You know, in case your mom's all mad and out looking for you. We'll just have to see."

"Maybe we could just call her later from a pay phone so she knows I'm okay."

"Yo, what you sayin', Bro?"

"I just don't want mom to be too upset."

"'Mommy, Mommy, Mommy. Listen to yourself! I told you, she has one and I have zero. She's had custody of you going on two years now. It's payback time."

"You mean we're not going back ever?"

"Why are you even talking like this? What kind of adventure is it when Tonto keeps boobing about wanting to sleep in his own little bed?" Adam's dad sighed loudly and flipped his cigarette butt out the window.

Adam played with the armrest between their seats until Russell told him to stop.

"How much further?"

"To the state line? Couple more hours."

"Are you still going to make me a rice-paper maze?"

"A what?"

"Remember? You said you were going to set up rice paper screens to make a maze in my bedroom if I wanted."

"I *did?* Where the hell am I going to get rice paper screens?"

"I don't know. And that we could bust out a wall if we had

to, to make room for the maze. You told me that on the phone yesterday."

"Oh yeah. Sort of. But listen, we have to talk about a few things."

"Like what?"

"Like if anyone asks you questions about where you're from. I really want this new living arrangement to work out but the fact is, until I can get your mother in a court of law and prove to the judge that I'm the more suitable and good parent, we're kind of going to have to lay low. Not answer too many questions. Like it wouldn't even be a bad idea if we came up with different names for each other. I don't know, that might kind of be going overboard. But maybe just until tonight, until we get there. It's not a big deal and anyway it might kind of even be fun. What do you think? If you could have any other name what would it be?"

"Spiderman?"

His dad guffawed. "Not Spiderman. A real name."

"I don't know."

"Well think about it, would ya? I want to stop and get a bite soon. How's about Jerry?"

"It sounds fake."

"*Jerry* sounds *fake?* Well, then you think of one. You just tell me and then when we go in restaurants and stores for the next couple of days, that's what we can call each other. And I think I'm going to shave this handlebar. Time to go incognito and clean-cut. Time for a new look."

"Are we hiding?"

Russell lit another cigarette. "You could call it that."

"What happens if the cops see us?"

"Nothing's gonna happen. A father's allowed to walk down

the streets with his son. But if you do see a cop, or if for any reason by any chance at all a cop ends up talking to you, you tell them your name. What's your name?"

"Adam Jarvis."

"No, your name is not Adam Jarvis. Your name is, what? Are you going to come up with one?"

"You mean a fake one?"

"Christ yes, a fake one. That's what I'm trying to communicate here."

"Elton Bartholomew."

His dad hooted. "Oh, now that is fancy. That is one fancy, faggoty name. How's about we just call you Charles Dickens, and you can just prance around in a top hat and tails? You kill me. 'Elton' is okay. Barely. But lose the rest. I'm Ray Smith, by the way. So you can be Elton Smith."

"Okay. Are we going to stop soon?"

"Sure. Let's stop. Let's eat. We can practice our new identities." Russell ground out his cigarette and patted Adam's hand. They were men, on the road and hungry.

At the restaurant they made a production of calling each other by their fake names and thinking up jokes and having a good old time. Then Russell went off to play the slot machines while Adam dawdled over a hot fudge sundae. It was eleven-thirty at night and his dad had said the border was only about two more hours away and after that, if Adam felt like it, they could go back to using their real names. But for now they were on an adventure.

The waitress came by and looked at him strangely and asked where his dad was. Adam just smiled and shrugged and dug up a large spoonful of ice cream. It was nobody's business. Then Russell came back and sat at the table and drank two beers, one right after the other.

"They sure have some weak shit-ass cocktails in this casino," he told Adam. "I've had three martinis and barely even got a buzz. I should just stick to Budweiser. You doing okay?"

"I'm okay."

"Want me to take you to the bar, where you can watch TV?"

"Sure."

They went to the bar and his dad had another drink and asked the bartender for a roll of quarters. Adam spun on the bar stool and rubbed at his eyes. Wherever his mom was now, she was crying. He thought about asking his dad again if they could call home but his dad had other things on his mind, like the twenty-eight dollars in quarters he'd lost in the slots. "I'm fixin' to recoup my losses before we get on the road again," Russell said. "That okay with you?" and Adam nodded.

The bar was shadowy and loud and after a while the bartender had brought him a bowl of unshelled peanuts and a 7UP. He watched football on the large screen and worked at the peanuts and waited. That was fine until he got too thirsty and needed to pee, but he didn't want to ask the bartender about where the bathroom was. His finger hurt badly and he held it in his glass of ice water, where the white bandage was a magnified cocoon. His butt hurt from the hard stool but he tried to be a man and not think about his bed and the sad warm smell of Menthol cigarettes and of his mother and of her warm yellow hair sliding, making them a tent where she breathed down on him and would smile. Adam felt his leg

twitch violently and realized that he'd almost fallen asleep,
which would be horrible if his dad saw that he couldn't even
stay awake the first night of their new life together. He splashed
some cold water on each eye and then practiced sliding his
water glass across the smooth counter like he'd seen the guy
slide a cool one down the bar on the Coors commercial. In
that commercial there were tall Texans and a jukebox and all
the people were laughing and dancing and beautiful women
tossed their beautiful curly hair and had very white teeth. He
thought of his mom again, and felt a warmth behind his eyelids, and placed a hand over his mouth to keep his lips from
trembling. If she hadn't taken the knife away, this never
would have happened. But he hoped his dad would come
back soon so that they could go on to Reno, and so that he
could sleep and then the next day see, when they were in
their new bright house, that there was a swimming pool out
back and a tire swing and a Ping-Pong table in the basement.
He put his head down on the bar, which sealed off one ear
and blocked out some noise. His mom was pushing him on a
tire swing and laughing. She was as pretty as one of the ladies
in the beer ad. She wore a pink halter top with lipstick to
match and she was saying something that he couldn't make
out. Adam slipped downward, and then his dad was driving
and driving and his dad's moustache was gone and he was
wearing a wig with all different colors, like a clown wig. He
reached his arm across to Adam and patted his back and
then started shaking him and when Adam opened his eyes
the bartender was stroking his hair and asking his name and
where did he live. Everything was foggy in his brain and he
heard himself saying his own name and phone number
plainly, the way his mom had taught him with the area code,

before realizing what he'd done. "I mean my name is Jerry," he said stupidly, but by then the bartender was at the phone, and giving him a thumbs-up for reassurance. "Seen kids like you before," he told Adam.

His dad appeared. "Didn't fall asleep did ya?"

"That guy woke me up."

"So you did fall asleep. Couldn't you stay awake for a lousy fifteen minutes? I gotta go back. Now I'm really in the hole. Boy oh boy, some sidekick. Some Tonto to my Lone Ranger. You really take the cheese."

"I'm sorry, dad."

"I know you're sorry. It's okay. We'll brush up on your constitution. You'll get used to staying up all night long if you want, before long, and then we can throw wild parties. You didn't tell him your name did ya?"

"I said Jerry," Adam said.

"You fucking better have."

"I *did*."

"I think little Jerry might need to hit the hay," the bartender said. He'd hung up the phone and was mopping the bar casually. "Are you staying the night?"

"None of your goddamn business," Russell said.

"Well now all I was going to say is, the cops never bug you if you want to park and sleep outside along them trees. That's what the truckers do. For that matter, I don't know what you think about this, but I've got a room voucher actually. Now and again the casino gives them out. If you want. It's just a regular room. Just a standard, but. It's got a TV and everything."

"Do I look like I need charity?" Russell said. "Do I look like some snaggle-tooth loser-ass unemployed alcoholic welfare case?"

"Nope. You don't," the bartender said. "Anyway. You really can just park over there."

"Well, thanks. Sorry I jumped your back. I thought I could win my money back before we had to get back on the road, but it was not to be."

"Happens to the best of us," the bartender said. "I've seen it before of course, working here. I've seen just about everything."

"I'll bet. That's probably not the first kid you've had sleeping at your bar," Russell said, and chuckled.

"It sure isn't. It sure is not."

"Well. I thank you kindly."

They went out to the car and his dad drove around to the trees and they parked alongside a blue semitruck. "People like that are just nosy," he said. "Did you see that guy? Like he was Mr. Seargent Fucking Friday. Mister how's about getting a real job for a change. 'Voucher.' Oh, that kills me. Like for free canned goods or something." His dad rolled up his jacket and passed it over to Adam. "What you gotta do is, you gotta outthink them," he said, and tapped his temple with a finger. "You gotta think, just exactly like a kung fu master, now what's this guy going to do? Where's he going to kick next? Is he going to give me a throat punch or get me in the nuts or just make some expert hai karate sound and thereby intimidate me into submission, or what? Like is he really mister tough guy or is he faking it? It's all about mind games or mind control or what have you. Do you understand?"

"Yes."

"Good," his dad said. "Put that in the memory bank and do not make a withdrawal."

"Okay. 'Night, Dad."

"Goodnight, John Boy. Jerry Boy."

The policeman appeared from out of nowhere. He rapped politely at his dad's window. "Could you step out of the car, please?"

"I didn't do nothing, Officer."

"Well then, just step on out."

"You stay here," his dad told him. Adam was shaking all over. Another policeman, this one a lady, slid into the backseat and addressed him: "You okay?" But Adam only zipped up his mouth and then threw away the key. "Okay," she said. "I see where you're at."

Adam started to cry when they put his dad in the other police car. At some point in the evening his dad had shaved and now he looked like a skinny, guilty teenager in his loose jeans and black T-shirt. He tried to turn to look at Adam but the cop pushed his head down to get him in the car, at which point his dad smacked his head and yelled "Well goddamn fuck!" and disappeared from view.

"Are you going to take me to jail?" Adam asked the lady cop. She was a black woman with a million braids all over her head. The cop smiled and shook her head no.

Adam watched the police car with his dad pull away. He wondered what they'd feed his dad in jail, and whether he could smuggle a file in inside a cake. But that would be in a perfect world, where his mom would drive him to the prison, dressed all in white and in a summer hat and carrying the cake in a large pink bakery box so that no one would guess what was hidden inside. And it would be a snowball's day in hell before she did that.

He stared out the window as they drove, not answering their

questions. Anyway they knew his real name; he'd already heard that much from over the radio. Images spooled by, signs and fenceposts and the dark shapes of closed buildings.

It was impossible—being himself. He realized—awfully—that he'd peed a little on his underwear, he'd been so scared. To keep the smell in he tucked his arms between his knees. He could hold it for quite a while longer. His mom always said when they drove places that he had a champion's bladder, the bladder of the world. She, on the other hand, always had to go. He thought of his mom, falling to her knees and crying huge tears when she heard that he was found, and his heart contracted with joy.

Mallory
the Cleaning
Lady

MALLORY THE CLEANING LADY was a gift from my husband, Bill. He was sick of hearing me bitch about all the housework, probably. Sick to be put to work himself the minute he stepped through the door. Our son, Dylan, was five, and his baby sister, Joy, was just two; and I was a permissive mother, open to all manner of science experiments and craft projects in the name of learning and creativity. We did dog kibble and hand lotion. We did pizza dough with nail polish, and potato chips with ketchup and grated cheese and lots of ice water. It was cute at first. But the kids grew, and before long there were yogurt stains on both sofas and grannies down the cracks of the couch and a large tic-tac-toe game drawn with a Sharpie on the white rug in the den. I'd gone back to work part-time, and had gotten to where I lectured Bill every time he so much as tried to read the paper over breakfast. *Do you see what I'm doing here?* I was liable to say. *You're sitting there reading, while I'm here loading the dishwasher.* So Bill talked to a guy he worked with, and paid Mallory in advance for six three-hour visits.

I mean this nicely when I say that I would've been more comfortable with a cleaning *team.* A team just seemed more anonymous, I guess. I liked the idea of a whole bunch of quiet people in uniforms who wouldn't meet my eye. A whole bunch of folks with squirt bottles who when the van pulled up to the curb would hop right out and move past me and come inside and do their work swiftly, soundlessly, and then leave again. But Bill read some article about how those companies actually did a really shitty job. How they just came in and fluffed the pillows and spritzed and just made it *feel* clean, instead of actually doing the cleaning on a microscopic level.

"I hope she's not just going to want to talk my ear off," I told Bill. It was ten o'clock, and we were in our king-sized bed,with a kid asleep on either side of us. Feel free to guess about our sex life. I knew there were other ways to parent, because we had friends who got their kids to bed by *seven.* But then, these parents had all read the same book about resolving their children's sleep problems; and in this book, the author exhorted parents to just put the kids to bed and ignore their hysteria at all costs. Even if the kid puked, *puked,* you were just supposed to efficiently and silently wipe it up and then leave them to cry it out again (!).

"You'll probably talk *her* ear off."

"I won't. I promise. It's going to be weird enough having somebody clean up after me. I'm going to *vanish.*"

"Aren't you excited about it?"

"Of course! I didn't mean that. Thank you for the cleaning lady. I'm sure she'll be great."

Bill kissed me, and his hands wandered. "Let's go in the kids' room and mess around."

"I'm not having sex in their room!"

"Well, where else?" Bill tried to climb over Joy and got her in the face with his elbow. She woke up shrieking. "Shit!" Bill said, and picked her up and rocked her a little. "Sorry, sweetheart."

"Anyway, since she's going to be here early, I want to get some stuff done. The house looks horrible. I'll be downstairs, okay?"

I went to the kitchen and poured myself a glass of apple juice. Then I stood looking at the refrigerator door, trying to think how it would look to a strange woman who'd come to clean my house. I'd been meaning to take a picture of the refrigerator door forever. It was archaeology; it was us. There were a lot of kids' drawings, especially Dylan's. He was famous for giving them good titles: *Egyptian Boy with Hat and Hands. Me and my skateboard at the cemetery. Aluminum alien underwear, belonging to an alien.* There were photos of the four of us, and a strand of milk tickets for Dylan's lunch, and a slew of postcards, and two weddings that still needed an RSVP, and several places where Joy had doodled with a tube of sparkly silver eyeliner. The rest of the kitchen wasn't much better: the table was our dumping ground for bills and homework and coupons, and also the place the kids and I did crafts. I opened the fridge. As tasks went, as preparation for the cleaning lady went, that one seemed reasonable. I would send the message that though my life was perhaps messy at first glance, I had higher priorities: gourmet cooking. Healthful snacks available for the children. Organic produce, imported beer.

But the fridge, the fridge it was not good.

There were many tubs of Tupperware, with food I didn't remember. There was margarine in a tub, instead of real butter, and a few broken and browning stalks of celery next to a pizza box, and part of a pot roast wrapped in foil. And lots of half-empty bottles of salad dressing, and a jar of unopened cocktail onions, and half-sandwiches and leftovers from Taco Bell still in their Taco Bell wrappers. There were shriveled lemons and several opened hot dog packages with one or two weenies missing from each. There were half-eaten apples, half-eaten bananas. The cap was long lost from the gallon of milk—it was *always* missing, though, really, how far could it go?—and a can of tuna wrapped so generously with foil that the bottom of the can was round, and the tuna sat at a tilt. It looked like the refrigerator of a housewife who'd long ago lost authority or interest. Me.

"Whatcha doing?" Bill bounded down the stairs. Everywhere he went, he moved like that. He was a man on the balls of his feet, a man in action. "Joy fell back asleep, by the way."

"Mallory starts tomorrow," I said.

"Yeah. So why are you cleaning?"

"Because, look at the fridge."

"The house looks fine. Have you been *cleaning?*"

"I did a little bit earlier. Just some straightening. Outta my way." I pushed past him to get to the garbage can. Then I changed the filter in the Brita water jug and dumped small carrots in a bowl of ice water so that a healthful snack would be right there for the taking. I arranged green apples in a white bowl, and stuck the rest of the apples in the crisper. I consolidated the many bags of cold cuts, turkey in one Ziploc and Swiss in another and ham in another, and displayed them nicely. Last, I made orange juice from concentrate and wiped hard-water spots from the clear-glass pitcher before transferring the orange juice into it.

I had many questions that I planned to ask Mallory once we got to know each other. Like, compared to other houses she cleaned, was ours really and totally the worst? Was ours the only one with rat poison under the sink? The only one where a dime had been mummified, and for almost a year now, on the kitchen floor, under several coats of Future floor wax? The dime was right there where anyone could see it. The kids had *contests*. They chiseled it with a screwdriver. "Move, please," I said to Bill, who was leaning against the stove, watching. "I'm gonna do the trash."

"This is nutty, look at you, you're nutty. That was the whole point of hiring her!" Bill said.

"Well I don't want Mallory doing *this*."

"Doing what? The trash? I'm pretty sure that's in her job description."

"Look at this. All of our beer bottles. I don't want her drawing conclusions."

"Actually, my beer bottles, your O'Doul bottles." Bill went looking in the fridge for a snack.

"Please don't touch those apples. Please. If you want one, get it out of the drawer."

"Why do you care if she sees your *nonalcoholic* beer bottles?"

"Because, Bill." I had to spell everything out for him. "If she sees those, she might think I used to have a drinking problem. Or think I'm pregnant and can't drink. Or that I'm Mormon, and you're not. Or—much more interesting—that we both used to be Mormon, only now one of us has fallen away from the church and so now drinks beer. I don't want her *speculating*."

Bill was looking at me intently. "Wow," he said. "It must suck to live in your brain some days."

I got the garbage can from under the sink and compressed the contents with my foot. "I can't believe she's going to be here at nine A.M.. I'm not even remotely ready. Could you take this out?" Finally the cylinder of garbage popped out, slimy and coffee-ground–encrusted. "It does, actually. Suck."

Like many people, I have had several ideas for making my First Million.

The first was a magazine called *Addiction*, featuring celebrities who've struggled with substance abuse. They would tell their stories. They would confess and enlighten. They would Tell All.

Second was a cleaning service that wouldn't make white middle-class people like me feel so bad. Sort of a starving-students thing. Philosophy majors with goatees. Girls with lip-piercings. And if they looked empowered, the girls especially, and scrubbed fast with their lithe tattooed bodies and could make something like scrubbing the bathroom floor, with its excitement of stray hairs and droplets, look subversive: well, that would be cool. Like if they were just doing it for the look, the irony, and not for the money. I hoped with all my heart that Mallory might be such a person.

I had applied for such a job, when I was an undergrad, at the U of A. There was an ad in the college newspaper about Helping with Women's Health. The phone interview went something like this:

—So, um, you understand what this is all about? You understand what you'd be actually doing in the job?

—I think so. Helping with women's health?

—Yes, with their reproductive health.

—Helping, like, to empower them? To empower us?

—Exactly. But you have to be sure you're up for it. Don't tell me you're going to show up if you won't, which I'm so sick of. I'm on commission here.

—I know.

—Whatever. So anyway, there's a speculum, you have to be brave, they're guys, they're first-year med, they stand around.

—They do the speculum on me? Wow.

—Exactly.

—For how much?

—Sixteen bucks an hour.

—Wow!

—I was hoping you'd say that.

—Are you serious?

—Are you chickening out?

—No.

I did. Chicken out. But that's another story.

But now I was just a white woman in the suburbs, about to have my whole house cleaned, this particular Tuesday morning, by Mallory. Maybe because I'd daydreamed about the subversive-looking housecleaning team, I actually thought such a thing was in place somewhere in the world. Maybe even in my own city. They'd all hop out looking sort of Goth and reading Goethe. They'd be cool. I wouldn't mind one bit, exchanging dark and clever quips while one of them scoured my sink.

Of course, I was still excited to have Mallory! This all makes it sound like I'm complaining. I wasn't complaining. She'd clean my house six times, and we'd go from there.

While she cleaned, I would clear out. I would—I would do things. Accomplish. Go places. Achieve, run errands. Move forward in life.

So. Mallory drove up. Since her car was such a piece of crap, I started feeling guilty and bad right away. I showed her in and showed her around. She was a large woman of few words, at least that first day. She was from Minnesota or some other state that started with an M. I knew that she worked two jobs, and worried she might be hungry. So I went to the kitchen and started making, of all things: banana bread.

I rarely cooked, let alone baked. It came out looking like a shoe.

"How was the thing with Mallory today?" Bill kissed me and poured himself a glass of wine. "Well, goddamn. Look at it in here!"

"I have to say, the floors look great. She even took the recycling over to the junior high. And look at the *counters*. I hung around for a while and tried to bake and befriend her, but I think I was kind of in the way, so I took the kids to the zoo. We had a great time, they were so cute. They wanted to spend practically the whole time in the reptile building."

"Wow, it really looks good." Bill was inspecting the kitchen floor. "She got the dime off!"

"She did?" I looked. Sure enough.

"Did she steal anything? Are our narcotics still intact?"

"No way! That's just an urban legend."

"What, that housekeepers steal? No it's not. Don't you remember a few years ago when that woman walked off with some of my mom's jewelry? Remember I told you that? Right before Dylan was born."

"Wow."

Dylan came in, dressed as a Ninja. Joy trailed behind. "Can we have ice cream?" Dylan wanted to know.

"Yay!" Joy went. She loved ice cream.

"She *kept* the dime?" Dylan said. "No fair!"

Maybe other women were able to just waltz off to the mall when their cleaning lady showed up. Not me. The following week, I made sure most of the really disgusting cleaning was done before she got there.

Still, I worried. I worried that Mallory might be sad and hungry and need an ear. I worried she might show up cold and shivering, and need a sweater. I worried she might need to be talked down from the ledge and offered a cigarette. I worried that she had her own house to clean, her own kids, her own *life,* and hated me for the fact that fortune had placed me thusly, in a position to pay *her* to clean up after *me.*

And I worried about her opinion of my life; because, say what you will, people cleaning your house are bound to notice things. They're going to notice what quality and color of matter is up under the rim, for example. They learn what you eat and what you secrete and what's in your medicine cabinet, and whether you recycle or are too lazy for even that. They know your vitamin supplements, expensive as they are, and they know the contents of your pockets, right down to receipts.

After only two visits, for example, Mallory knew that I sat on the edge of my bed to clip my toenails, and that I stock-piled Monistat 3 and drooled on my pillowcase at night. She knew, much worse, the various hues of my body hair, apparent as they were in the shower drain. She knew the smell of our bedroom in the morning. I was worried from Day

One that I would not make a good impression, either in terms of my people skills or my personal hygiene. And it was exactly this that drove me into a frenzy in the hours before she arrived.

I wanted her to *like* cleaning our house, or at least like us. I wanted her to like the smell of it, and to feel free to wander out into our yard and pick cherries from our tree, though I'd only be happy about this if the lawn were mowed and the dog poop scooped, and the toys cleared from the patio and the patio swept and hosed and finally made shiny with sealer I'd picked up at Home Depot, making our patio look, for once in its life, like a place of respite and spiritual refreshment; a place with bird feeders (needing to be filled), chaise longues (the cushions in need of a wash), and redwood planters brimming with healthy perennials (Slug-Be-Gone squirted around the edge; a quick trip to Home Depot for more gerber daisies to replace those Dylan and Joy had picked, in a rush of love and in about ten seconds flat, as the gift of a bouquet to: me); an actual place where people like me, *people who had money to pay a cleaning lady,* went to *relax.* I wanted her to know our family life might be chaotic but that that didn't preclude attention to safety, which translated to needing new springs and pads for the trampoline. Oh, I wanted Mallory to know *lots* of things: I wanted her to know that I knew there were poets in the world whose work she'd appreciate, but most possibly not be familiar with, which led to the strategic placement of certain poems on the fridge. I wanted her to know that we did laundry, and often and in a timely fashion, and so took to piling the excess laundry in garbage bags I tossed in a hall closet, instead of leaving it in the usual mound on the bathroom floor. I wanted her to know that I folded my underwear before I put it away, at least now that I had a cleaning lady. I wanted there to be coffee, and coffee *cake,* on hand to offer for when she showed up.

I wanted her to know that although I could afford her, for at least six visits, I *cared.* And the only way I could do this— *obviously,* unless I wanted to do it all myself—was to ride herd. Bill was watching *Queer Eye for the Straight Guy* when I found him in the den.

"Could you straighten back here before you come up to bed?"

"How come? Isn't Mallory coming tomorrow?"

See? He really saw it that way.

"She is, but I don't want her to see it looking like *this.* Like we *live* this way. Look at that, what is that? Is that a cottage cheese container on the couch? See what I *mean?*" I was already getting pissed. I stomped over to pick it up myself. There was still cottage cheese in it, but the lid was nowhere in sight.

"I don't. Actually."

"It looks like we're pigs. Like we're the kind of people who eat whatever the hell, all over the house. Oh my God," I'd spotted a bunch of Kotex over by the bookcase. "Fuck! Were the boys playing with these again? Why are these all open?"

"They were taping them on their feet to play soldier."

"What?"

Finally, Bill peeled his eyes away from the Fabulous Five. "Soldier," he said. "Playing. Wearing your pads. Because they stick them to the bottom of their feet."

"Why would soldiers need to parade around with Kotex taped to their feet? See, this is my point. She's going to show up tomorrow and have to clean up a box of some other woman's Kotex, and she is going to have questions in her brain."

"They needed them to skate across the moat. They slide better on the carpet, and there were alligators, also boa constrictors I guess, in the moat. Want me to show you how it works?"

"I just wish you'd see it from my angle once in a while."

"What? Why am I in trouble? For getting you, as a present, a cleaning lady? Please tell me this is not my beautiful life."

"Because, A, now she knows my choice of feminine protection. Just for starters. Even though it's *not*, even though I'm in fact hip, and use tampons and don't even fucking use ones with applicators. So see, if I don't clean them *up*," I was hurling them one after another into the trash—"she will think I am a pad-wearer. She will never know, our Mallory, that these are left over from when I gave birth and was bleeding and leaking all over myself."

"At least they're not *used* ones."

"Are you going to help me here? Because I am just feeling totally pissed off right now. Just pick up the rest of the sticky papers. I'll get these."

"Okay, I kind of get why you care about the pads."

We cleaned together. I liked nothing better, I swear, than for us to be cleaning or doing some house project together. I couldn't help it. Otherwise, he talked while I did puny, unnoticed chores on the periphery. When I'd completed that chore, I went to the bookcase, which led to the yanking out of several incriminating books. "Could you please get me that empty Fruit Gushers box on the porch?"

"Why? What are you doing? You look insane. You should see your hair. You look like bipolar Dorothy."

"I *feel* insane! I'm putting these books away, what else do you think I'm doing!"

"*Why*?"

"You know what? Because, Bill. Because. Look at these. I

don't want her seeing these. Look," I spread them out on the floor: *the Kama Sutra, the Couple's Guide to Getting Your Groove Back. Sick and Tired of Being Sick and Tired. The Joy of Sex*, an edition from the 1970s that I'd bought way back when not only because the illustrations were such a crack up, but because there was actually a page or two—in the section on lesbian sex—devoted to *tucking*; which, according to this edition, was a method of foreplay exclusive to lesbians. And tucking was what it sounded like. In the illustration, a woman with an afro *tucked* her lover into bed. Then they turned off the light and went to sleep.

"Who cares if she knows we have a sex life?"

"You know what, please just get me the box. I beg of you."

"Am I going to have to spend my whole evening cleaning for the cleaning lady?"

"I don't want her to know our sex life sucks! I don't want her to form opinions! I just want her to clean! That's why I liked the idea of a team!"

Bill removed himself with dignity. He went to the kitchen and returned with a beer, his head held at the sad angle it was when I'd hurt his feelings. "Sorry," he said. "Sorry I didn't get you a *team*."

"Oh, stop. I didn't mean that. I'm sorry. I do like having Mallory, I do. I'm sorry."

"Didn't you hear about that study? The one where they looked at the room with ultraviolet light and found jism on everything. Even on the ceiling. All over other people's walls."

"I think that was that 20/20 thing on hotel rooms. How there was sperm on everything, even the remotes."

"I can sort of see, with the remotes. My point is I thought

she would clean the house better. And that's the point, right? For *her* to clean the house. Julie and Brian recommended her. I don't get why you're feeling all this, not like rich people give a shit. They just let other people clean and mow and slave all around them."

"Exactly. Exactly!" I said.

"But we're paying her. She *wants* this job."

"I know. I'm just a freak."

"If Mallory isn't *helping*, then let's just tell her we don't need her anymore. It was supposed to be a present."

"I *know*. I don't know how to explain it. She gets here, and I feel like I have to do things. Help her clean, or prove I have some other important life that necessitates a cleaning lady. I can't just get on the treadmill or watch daytime television while she cleans all around me."

"We're paying her!"

And I kept trying to explain it to him; hoping that if I talked enough, and long enough, it would all come clear.

"The thing is, the house is my workplace. It's like you with MicroDyne. You go there to work. You do it because that's where you *work*. It's your *job*. So when Mallory shows up, it's like I'm at work, and then she stands there and does my job right in front of me. Like if somebody just waltzed into your office and sat down and started doing your job on the computer."

"Can't you just clear out?"

"And go where? Shopping? Come home with bags of stuff she can't afford and then show them to her?"

"Maybe you could take the kids somewhere. The park or something."

The thing I liked about Bill was: when there was no right

answer, when there was no possible way he could win, he kept right on trying. He was just an optimist. He had this sweetness. Bill was the kind of guy who would pick up the phone when a telemarketer called, and listen to a recorded message that said *we have an important message for you! Please wait for the next available agent.*

And he *would.*

"You could take them to your mom's for a few hours, and then go sit in a coffee shop and read a book. It's supposed to be a good thing. A good and happy thing, that we can afford to pay someone to clean our house. Are any valuables missing, by the way? Not that we have any."

"It's not personal. Do you get that it's not personal? It's just, like, the whole system. The whole housewife, suburbs, husband-working-to-support-us thing. I know your job sucks. I know the kids won't be little forever. I know we'll eventually have a sex life and go places like France. It's just *now,* and I feel like such an ingrate to not even appreciate her. Maybe I should just go back to work full-time. And you could stay home."

"Except that I make three times more than you did. Sadly."

"Yep," I said. "There's the rub. You make enough that we can even afford a cleaning lady. I just don't know how much longer I can do this." I flattened the empty Kotex box and held it out. "Could you stick this in the recycling?"

By Mallory's third visit, I'd persuaded her to sit down and chat for a while, before starting to work. I couldn't stand the thought of her walking in and just starting to *clean.* It seemed like there should be more of a warmup between us, more of a getting-to-know-you period. So usually we'd at least have coffee first. It was probably wrong to encourage it so much, I knew. She was being paid by the hour. But I did the same thing with my psychologist, tried to get her talking. I couldn't figure out if it was passive–aggressive or pathological or what. It was *something*.

All I knew was that I was most comfortable when I was trying to prove myself to her. On top of coffee hour, I'd also started to think up errands for her to run, and errands that she would *like*: trips to Bath and Body Works, where I wanted Mallory to buy extra hand lotion for herself. Jaunts to the bookstore, the candy store, the gourmet food market, where I urged her to pick up an extra log of goat cheese. It was like I was on TV all the time, rehearsing: *this is what a housewife with a conscience looks like, this is what a good wife and mother does for her employees.* Because I didn't even *like* Mallory. She wore clothes I wouldn't be caught dead in, cardigans with shoulder pads and jeans with elastic waistbands. She painted her fingernails in stripes, with the colors of our local basketball team. She had no sense of humor, at least that I could detect; and when I broached the subject of poetry she shut me down fast, saying she hated depressing poetry. So why I sucked up to her was anybody's guess. And the fact that I wasted my time sucking up to her, the fact that I disliked her but still tipped her lavishly and shared my favorite poems—poems that *meant* something, that had *changed my very life*, that were resonant and heartbreaking, and so beautifully done that they made me want to collapse in front of the fridge and weep and pound the floor—those, Mallory made short work of.

"How come none of your favorite poems ever *rhyme?*" she'd ask flatly.

If there was fresh coffee, she accepted it. She went to the mall without enthusiasm, and obediently handed over my change when she returned. She did what she was asked, whether it was scouring the countertop or making the beds or agreeing to a refill. I wanted to believe that still waters ran deep, but each new glance at Mallory's pie-pan face shook my faith. If anything, my attentiveness bothered her; when finally I took my coffee cup to the sink her relief was apparent. She'd exhale loudly and escape for the cleaning caddy.

"I can't figure her out," I told Bill as we were getting into bed. I moved Dylan carefully over so I could have my own pillow. "It's like she has no personality."

"She's just our cleaning lady. You probably bug her. You're probably sort of in her personal space."

"*I'm* in *her* space?" Joy stirred, waking up, and we both froze. Then she settled back, breathing through her mouth.

"Is she doing a good job?"

"She does a really good job. She's great. I just don't know what's going on in her head. I mean, what does she think of us?"

"Who cares?"

"I kind of do. I'm kind of interested. I wonder what her house looks like."

"Probably an apartment. A small one. With a cat. And I'll bet she watches a lot of TV."

"See, but I hate to stereotype that way. Maybe she's a sex addict. Maybe she has a master's in philosophy."

Bill rubbed his eyes. "Can I turn the light off?"

"You really don't care, do you? About the cleaning lady's rich inner life."

"I'm just glad we've only paid her for three more times. Good riddance." Bill turned off the light and climbed over Dylan so we could cuddle. "*You* clean the bathroom next time."

• • •

The morning of Mallory's fourth visit, I packed up my gym bag and even got the car idling. When she arrived, I was a Woman Ready. "I'm going to do a little bit of running around," I told her. "I have my phone, if you need anything."

"Okay."

"You can have the TV on if you want. I usually like it on when I clean. And of course, whatever you want to eat or drink."

"You're too nice to me," Mallory said. "You should just treat me like more of an employee. You're paying me, remember. I don't just show up for shits and giggles."

"I know that," I said. "There's also a new bag of Halloween candy. Snickers. And please make sure you take fifteen-minute breaks at least."

Mallory scowled. "I'm only here a whole three hours."

"Still, if you were working like in a store, you'd be required by law to take breaks. Okay?"

Mallory rolled her eyes. "Okay. Sure."

"I mean, I don't have to insist on this."

"You just get so much up in your own *face*," Mallory said suddenly. "It's painful to watch."

I pretended to look for my jacket. Fuck her. She was a freak. "Suit yourself," I said.

"I mean, you're paying *me*."

"I know that."

"I just think the next couple of weeks would be easier. If you stopped trying. Trying to impress me and prove you have some big heart." Mallory was rummaging under the sink and noisily plonking cleaning supplies onto the floor. "Just let me do my job, okay? I swear that's why I hate working for women. You have to always *talk* and *talk* about things."

"Mallory!" I felt like I was going to start crying. "What the hell! Did you get dumped this morning or something?"

"I'm just having a shitty fucking day," Mallory said. "I'm sick of this whole career. All of this guilt, guilt guilt you feel toward me. I'm surprised you don't clean alongside me, that's what a lot of them do." Mallory reached into her jacket and pulled out a pack of cigarettes. She tapped one out and lit up. "You even put the same poems on the fridge. William Carlos Williams. That plums-in-the-icebox thing."

"Please don't smoke in here."

Mallory looked me in the eye and blew a few smoke rings.

"What did I ever do to you? Fine then, don't take breaks. Don't eat. I just feel bad, because you're cleaning my house."

"Exactly," Mallory said, pointing her cigarette at me. "Bingo. And therein lies the dilemma of the system." She ground out her cigarette. On the *floor*. Why she hated me so much right then, I couldn't tell you. I stood there in my yoga pants and tank top, just trying to make sense of about the last thirty seconds of my life. "Fuck you for this," I said, and plucked up the butt. "That's just a really lovely gesture."

"Yeah, well fuck you for your whole stupid life," Mallory said. "You think I *like* changing your dirty sheets? I'm going." She took her blue denim shoulder bag from the chair.

"Please do," I said. My voice was small. She slammed out, and I heard her car start up. Who wore yoga pants, anyway? Besides me. They made me feel vulnerable. They showed my cleft.

I blew my nose and fished through the trash, looking for Mallory's old cigarette. As always I felt under surveillance, a housewife with her feelings hurt, a homemaker trying to work the childproof lighter. I could be seen folding laundry at two o' clock, doing Pilates on the living room floor at three. I could be seen from every angle, mopping and scrubbing and making public, making always public, the life of my lemony-scented home. My abdominal area was called a Powerhouse. My kitchen counters were reasonably germfree, even without Mallory's help. Somewhere on the planet a woman scrubbed her own pot, just one, and turned it upside down and left it in the sun to dry. She was calmer than me, and thought nothing of chopping the head off a chicken if that was what needed doing. She worked steadily, a large solid presence with children at her ankles. She wore wooden shoes.

Some Body Parts
Remember a War

A WOMAN WITH TEETH, with teeth, with hair. A stage singer, and when she sang her legs rolled like water like she had no kneecaps plus she wore a shiny blue man's silk suit and underneath it, without kneecaps, those crazy hoppin' rollin' legs drove you wild with happiness. And all around you were girls who loved her just the same as you; who threw roses onstage and blew kisses and held their chests like their hearts would bust right out. Like they were at a Beatles concert maybe. But the woman just sang and sang, smiling sexily now and then like she was thinking of somebody, and you and everybody in the audience could see it. Try to imagine them, the stage singer with dark hair glistening and high and spiky on her head and some woman, blonde, wearing a bright plastic red lei. Walking. Holding hands. Kissing. Her knees rolled! She galloped across the stage, still singing, and then slid right onto her side like someone coming into homeplate!

She was still singing lying there flat on her back and who knows what might've occurred to her looking up into those hot humongous white lights.

Well, and the crowd went wild. And the singer sat up, combed her hair flat with her fingers, hit a long low note, a most amazing long low note; then propped herself up on one elbow and noticed a child sleeping in the audience. So the singer stood up and walked to the edge of the stage and said to the dad of the little girl: *did we lose her?* And the little girl who'd fallen asleep with arms and hair hanging back now looked like a corpse against her dad's chest, even amongst the screaming loving fans who threw so many piles of roses, swaddled in cellophane, enormous and crackling. The singer had to step around them the way you step around doo-dahs on a miniature golf course.

What you do next is go to Lake Tahoe where she has her next concert and you're wearing red tights, the reddest tights of all, with pale green cowboy boots that don't match but who cares since this, this giving over and giving in to her, is surely the purest joy you've ever known. Walkin' in those boots makes your hips swing! Find the casino she's staying in. Write to your friends, say: I've never heard such a thing! as the way the notes came out of her mouth. As the way her mouth moved around in her face like she was eating canaries and angels all at the same time. Oh, my. Your brother tells you on the phone she is terrible-looking, why doesn't she at least wear some earrings. Think of all the self-mutilations you've seen, in magazines and real life: your own earlobes, a woman in a biker magazine who'd pierced her genitals. The woman wore a silver hoop and a chain, which was held by a hand at the edge of the photograph. She was smiling, looking proud.

Get off the phone and wait in the lobby, hoping to get a glimpse of her. The bellhop has fallen in love with you. He has no idea. He admires your tights. He admires your red nails. He knows things about the singer, like that she's on the sixteenth floor and a very friendly person, a very genuine person he says, though he has never seen her sing and howl and slide, never seen the roll and sweep of this same singer's legs. He has never noticed maybe such straight white teeth and cheekbones which give her appearance an Aleut cast, that's what you think, or even sort of a fetal cast. What you mean is her features are smooth and low-lying, like she wasn't quite through growing into her face before she got born. Try to explain this to the bellhop. He says *fetal?* He touches one of your red fingernails, finally gets around to snapping the red nylon bunched over one kneecap after you waited on the couch in the lobby three hours, hoping for a glimpse.

On the street you have never felt so good, so beautiful so madly in love and it makes you strut, the skies in Lake Tahoe are chlorine blue and a man sees you on the street. He's tromping toward you on the sidewalk, his boots sinking in snowdrifts and when you come even the man says *Do you work for the casino?* He says *How much?* The way you'd been smiling so big! The way you'd worn red tights just for the singer! Give him the birdie. But later, change into sedate panty hose.

Send a letter up to the singer's room the morning of her second and last appearance in beautiful Lake Tahoe. Invite her to breakfast! At Denny's, tell the waitress: Two. The singer never shows up. Her legs roll and roll. Feel it in the place where you think your womb must be, though hard to know for sure.

Wait again in the lobby. Then here comes the singer: watch how she holds the heavy glass door for a blonde-haired woman carrying a huge plant. The singer, trying not to be noticed, makes a beeline for a red velvet sash beyond which is the auditorium. Your legs huff and puff getting to her though the trick is not to scare her off by seeming like a loony-tunes fruitcake who could whip out a pistol any second. It happens to lots of celebrities and you're pretty sure she worries about it since why wouldn't she? But oh. But oh. Because now she's trapped behind the red sash, the auditorium door is locked so she's going to be looking at you any second. When she turns to say *what* in a tired voice, she's had it with adoring fans, remember lines from *The Waste Land*, remember: *I could not speak, I was neither living nor dead and I knew nothing. Nothing.* Remember, *looking into the heart of light, the silence.* Then the singer gets impatient, she says, *What!* This is when you realize she doesn't love you, can you believe it? Though since you first heard her songs it was like having a tiny invisible giraffe friend that hung out in your pocket who you were always trying to think up jokes for. See with shame that you're keeping her friend with the plant from even being able to escape to the elevators. Oh goodness the embarrassment and grief. Nothing can come out of your mouth. You can't even say I'm sorry.

One year later World War III happens. Rock-n-roll with the singer in secret love and privacy in your living room all the months in between. Catch an interview between the singer and Connie Chung where Connie wears earrings and tells the singer she dresses like a man. Catch the footage of missiles sailing through black skies into Iraq. On television no one will say how many people are dead, instead they say our objectives have been satisfactorily achieved. She is a singer and has nothing in common with war and only instead with your vanity; but somehow both things, the memory of her mouth and now the bodies flying, get you in the same way. Because anymore you can't tell where your heart is or find your own brain or even your own bowels. At some point, maybe that day in the casino or maybe these days watching Dan Rather's mouth, all the parts seem to have come loose and floated away from their moorings. At some point all the organs and bones remembered something and, without asking, switched places. You could wake up tomorrow and find a kidney on your tongue. Find a kneecap scooting along your spine, trying to get home. Catch the footage of more missiles making humongous white holes in a daytime sky. Catch the corpses. Think: *lost, lost, we've lost her, all.*